Angel Girl and the Hawk

Angel Girl and the Hawk

Secrets of the Cold War

A Novel

Samara Anjelae

ISBN: (Paperback) 978-1-7341509-2-6
ISBN: (ebook) 978-1-7341509-7-1
Published in the United States by Freebody Press.
www.freebodypress.com

Front cover image by Robin Hamon
Book cover design by Carolyn Austin
Formatting by Polgarus Studio

Disclaimer:
Angel Girl and the Hawk is a work of fiction. Names, characters, businesses, places, events, and incidents are either the products of the author's imagination or used in a fictitious manner. Any resemblance to actual persons, living or dead, or actual events is purely coincidental. Certain long-standing institutions, agencies, and public officials are mentioned, but the characters involved as well as their relationship to said institutions should be assumed imaginary.

To all the unsung Roberts of the world who live a life in service as warriors in the battle of good and evil, and to all the angels that guide and protect them.

Contents

"If it's necessary, it's legal."

General Thomas W. Buckley
National Security Agency Director, 1952

The National Security Agency accomplished a nearly impossible feat by staying invisible since its inception in 1952, when President Truman signed a memo creating the most secretive espionage unit ever established. Its mandate was simple yet straightforward: gather useful information for the Department of Defense intelligence community. Only the sitting president and a handful of generals were privy to the agency dubbed the "No Such Agency." Congress, White House staff including the vice-president, and the American public had no knowledge that this agency existed.

Within this secret agency, a secret division was later created called Covert Operations. Initially an experiment, it grew into an elite group of undercover operatives: super-warriors and psychics. The NSA was on the leading edge of using paranormal resources with top-secret spy missions.

By the mid-seventies, the NSA was on its way to becoming the largest federal agency in history, both in budget and personnel. Undocumented and unaccountable to Congress, thousands of employees worked in the computer department as scientists, programmers, technicians, and information analysists. Most NSA employees knew nothing about the secret branch. Covert Operations offices were deep underground at NSA headquarters in Fort Meade, Maryland. The dark operatives, and the Paranormal Research Department, commonly referred to as the Spooks, called their headquarters Neptune.

These exclusive and specially trained agents didn't have to live by the law on American or foreign soil. If the President of the United States sanctioned a mission, it was legal because it was necessary. Active generals served as the director and assistant director of the department. They had the authorization to spy on anyone, including the FBI and CIA. In some instances, they even spied on the President and White House.

During the Cold War, the NSA was cognizant that the only way to continue to be the pre-eminent spy organization was to recruit viable candidates. To accomplish this, incognito agents visited distinguished schools, laboratories, and businesses throughout America. It was typical to find them at Harvard, Yale, Stanford, MIT, as well as at DuPont, Fairchild-Hiller, Westinghouse Electric, Bell Labs, or just about anywhere that led them to the best of the best.

Angel Girl and the Hawk chronicles the recruitment and careers of the covert branch's top field agent and their most proficient psychic.

Help

"Help. Please help! It's Tuck. Tuck. You have to tell them now. My team is down. Six dead."

It was a desperate-sounding voice, not a voice from an angel. I heard it by thought. Within seconds, I had left my meditative state, trembling and breathing like I was inhaling death.

Who is this? Who is this voice I'm hearing?

I turned off my music and grabbed a legal pad from my desk. I was scared, nervous; nothing like this had happened to me before. As the voice talked, I saw pictures in my mind, like an action scene in a movie—I struggled to take notes—everything was moving so fast. I was in an old hotel, a brothel house, with lots of little rooms and a large parlor. There was one titanic room with a grand piano, sofas spread everywhere, velvet drapes and a massive, winding staircase with carpet and oak railings that led to a mezzanine. It was dark, nighttime. Men surfaced on the balcony with mammoth rifles. I heard the sound of pop, pop, pop, pop …

Tuck's thoughts continued to come through. "I'm dead. I need your help. Robert is …"

Robert! Oh God! Not my Robert.

I frantically spoke out loud to the distressed spirit, as if it were standing physically in front of me.

"What about Robert? Robert who? Tuck, who are you?"

"Team's lead, Robert's down and two others. They need to evac immediately."

I saw the picture in slow motion. Soldiers taking many rounds of bullets, their bodies jumping in violent, spasmic motions. It was like watching puppets shaken viciously, strings swiftly slashed, and falling instantly to the ground. I flashed to a collapsed soldier on the floor, motionless, blood covering his head and face. He appeared dead. It was Robert. I dropped my pad and pen, fell to my knees and tried to breathe. My connection with Tuck had grown fainter, much static, similar to tuning into a radio channel out of range. I didn't know if Tuck was still with me, or if I was hearing multiple voices, or had lost my mind.

"Tuck, if you can hear me, I'll get help." I was so confused with the information and how I received it that I had to dial Gloria's number three times before I got it correct. I couldn't even concentrate on my name. Sally? Rose?

Gloria answered on the third ring. "What's wrong? Rose, you sound terribly upset?"

"Robert may be dead or dying!"

"Calm down, what happened?"

"I was meditating, and a dead person came through. A discarnate. Said his name was Tuck, and to get help. Our team ambushed. Soldiers dead. South America, maybe. This is crazy, I don't know a Tuck."

Gloria came over promptly. She lived only a few cottages away. I prayed incessantly as I changed out of yoga clothes into jeans and a sweater. I summoned my angels and any help I could get until she arrived. Gloria decided it would be best that we talk to David in person. He lived off base, but it was only a ten-minute ride. While David was not gifted, he adamantly believed in those who were.

WE ARRIVED AT DAVID'S house and he listened to the sequence of events. He said I had had a hybrid paranormal experience. Mediumship with a fallen soldier and remote viewing of the location and setting. Although he had never dealt with this before, he knew if I was accurate, time was critical. He placed an urgent call to the assistant director of covert operations, General Lang.

General Lang confirmed there was a Commander Tucker Anderson in Bogota, Columbia, and that Robert Sexton was part of that unit.

Gloria, David, and I headed to Neptune to await intel.

She Talks to Angels

The words didn't seem to be real at first: "For God's sake, Sally Olivia Stone, you don't have a chance in hell in becoming an actress."

I hung up the phone. *She's supposed to be happy for me, not try to discourage me.* My mother just didn't know how to be a mom. Since the airing of the NBC special on angels, *Beyond the Light*, I'd been inundated with phone calls. Being in the company of George Harrison and Carlos Santana had opened up doors and created more choices with my career. I wasn't used to receiving so much attention. But in my mother's eyes, I was still a problem child who lived in a make-believe world.

In one week I would be graduating, a year early and with honors: *summa cum laude*. It was a waiting game to see if I got the part in *Charlie's Undercover Angels,* a drama that followed the crime-fighting adventures of three psychic women who worked in a private detective agency. I had auditioned for the role of Kelly Garret, one of the psychics.

The phone rang. I almost didn't answer, afraid it might be my mother again.

"Hello, Sally, two guests are in the lobby that'd like to speak to you. They say they're scouts from a talent agency."

My spirits lifted to a better mood.

"Tell them I'll be right there." I put down the phone and looked in the mirror. I threw on some blush and lip-stick, brushed and pulled back my hair, and quickly changed into my favorite plaid Ralph Lauren button-down and a long pleated skirt. I proceeded out the door at my usual fast-paced walk. It was exciting to have talent scouts visit me at Ole Miss, but surprising that they showed up without contacting me first.

My guests were easy to pick out. One was a nice-looking man, forty-fiveish, in a black fitted suit, wearing a wide-brim fedora and carrying a film reel in his hand. As I approached, the woman, strikingly lean with long, curly, dark hair, reached out and shook my hand. I couldn't help but notice how impeccably dressed she was. She wore a tight chartreuse pencil skirt that clung to her shapely legs, and a matching jacket with a fern blouse. A scarf, accessorizing her outfit, made her big green eyes pop. She was attractive enough to be a movie star herself.

In an animated tone, she said, "Hello Sally, I'm Gloria Childers."

"And I'm Anthony Grogan." He was soft-spoken and had a strong handshake. "Sally, we saw you on the angel show, and we'd like to talk to you about your professional choices. We think you have the potential for a wonderful future. We realize you're close to graduating and have many career opportunities. Let's walk over to the library where we can talk in private. We reserved the audio-visual room, where we won't be disturbed."

I agreed but wondered how they knew I was free and had no classes. The brisk walk through The Grove was short and casual; you could hear faint echoes of the "Hotty Toddy" chant from the nearby track field. Once we were in the room and settled in our chairs, Anthony pulled out a thin leather wallet and flashed a badge.

"Sally, we're not entertainment agents, we work for the government.

We're with the National Security Agency. NSA. You've never heard of us; no one has. We're a top-secret organization …"

He continued to talk but his words seemed to run together because my mind was racing. *Am I in trouble? Have I done something wrong? Oh my God! Is my mother behind this?* Then I heard him say, "Gloria is a psychic like you. She's our best paranormal intelligence source and has been on our team for eleven years. We've studied and researched you, and we believe you'd be another valuable asset like her."

Suddenly I was able to listen closely. I didn't know if I was more excited about being approached by a secret government agency, or more disappointed they weren't talent scouts. Either way, this was not an ordinary day.

"You may be working on a book, or a screenplay, or considering television," said the well-dressed psychic. "All those things are possible, but we believe that if you joined our organization, you could be a part of our family and make a difference in people's lives." Gloria leaned toward me. "You hold more power than you realize. You're a healer as well, and that may manifest in time. For now, we could nurture, grow, and expand your abilities."

I was a bit perplexed about having "power," and more puzzled as to how the agency used psychics. Many questions and scenarios ran through my mind. Gloria and Anthony attempted to answer them during the hour without giving away classified information. They shared that some of their responsibilities included protecting presidents, congressmen, senators, and visiting heads of state. Imagine a Russian ambassador assassinated on US soil, for example, could trigger World War Three.

Gloria revealed that when CIA, FBI, or NSA personnel were engaged in various activities, they often used a psychic as a resource to best accomplish their goals. They were consulted on such things as when to fly, the route to take, which door to open, and even used their insight as to the feasibility of an overall plan.

"From one clairvoyant to another, you haven't even begun to reach the limits of your ability. If you come on board with us, you'll be introduced to paranormal behaviors you may be unaware of. You'll grow more in six months with us than you could in six years on your own. You'd be surprised how often people like you and I are involved in crucial situations and decision-making.

"As for your work schedule, it's a pretty good one. Lots of travel, lots of time off, and good pay. But the real reward isn't financial; it's the gratification that comes from the work you do. Sally, I hope you consider joining our team. I would enjoy working with you."

Anthony, speaking seriously and evenly, said, "You certainly aren't expected to make a decision today. Give it some thought. We ask that you don't talk to anyone about this: your parents in Kentucky, Luke, Reba, or Thomas, your friends, or your sorority sisters."

They had the names of my siblings, where my parents lived, details that were never shared on the show. *How did they know?*

"And now," said Anthony, "you're probably wondering how we know this much about you. We're NSA. We know everything. It's our job. If you're interested in our proposal, we'll arrange for you to come to our headquarters. After our initial meetings, you'll begin a one-month trial period to make sure that both you and the agency feel it's a suitable fit. If you decide to take this role, you'll be making a contribution to science and humanity." Anthony ended with a JFK quote: "Ask not what your country can do for you; ask what you can do for your country."

Gloria handed me a card with her phone number. "It has been a true pleasure to meet you in person. If you have any questions, you can contact me any time. I look forward to hearing from you. I'll follow up with you in several days ..."

After a moment's hesitation, I decided I had better interrupt and tell her I'd been approached for a possible job. "I was flown out last week to read for a part in a new television series. I'm waiting to hear back from the producer. He said he'd be in touch as soon as he completes the rest of the auditions."

Gloria smiled. "Yes we know about Aaron Spelling Productions and that sounds very promising, but I want to leave you with these words to think about: 'You can make money, or you can make a difference.'" We walked back to my dorm. All I could think about was the "No Such Agency," and the meaning of Gloria's departing words.

I LAY ON MY BED, motionless, confusion in my mind. The dorm hallway was unusually loud. My warm hands rested on my stomach, like a heating pad bringing comfort to a sick soul. I was unable to differentiate between my thoughts and what were psychic, intellect, or just imagination. I wished I had someone to turn to who could help me think things through. My whole life I had made decisions on my own, quick decisions, and taken risks, significant risks. Growing up in the Crazy Stone house forced me to be independent and self-reliant. There was nothing holding me back, no love or boyfriend in my life. My mother was probably right. I wasn't Hollywood material. While acting sounded much more glamorous than working for the government, the idea of joining a clandestine agency appealed to my Scorpio nature. It reminded me of my favorite childhood book, *Harriet the Spy.*

Night seemed to fall early. In my bedtime prayer, I asked the Almighty Creator, God, to answer two simple questions: *Who am I,* and, *What do you want of me?* I went to sleep early even though my roommate still had the light on and was studying. During the night I woke up several times and fell back to sleep. I dreamed I was on a small wooden boat and drifting gently out to sea. No one else was around, just me, God, and the ocean. The boat was riding a wave when I saw the sea foam on the blue spell out the words, *"live, love, and make a difference."* I opened my eyes. The clock read 5:55 a.m. Decision made.

At 6:05 a.m. I dialed the phone, "Hello, Gloria, this is Sally."

It Takes Two

MY PARENTS WERE A NO-SHOW FOR MY COMMENCEMENT ceremony. The Grove, where commencement took place, never looked more beautiful. Clear skies, sunshine, and the canopy of trees—elm, oak, magnolia—that provided just the right amount of shade. My graduation fell on Mother's Day, and my mother had no intention of coming to Oxford when it was supposed to be her day to receive acknowledgment and accolades. It wasn't too surprising. Still, I was sad. Support and acceptance were a foreign trait in our family.

TWO WEEKS AFTER GRADUATION

My driver, an army officer, approached the guarded gate at Fort Meade. He nodded to the heavily armed Marines who nodded back and simply let us pass. The fort looked like a huge business complex except for the unusual amount of uniformed military walking around. Many men were wearing suits. I had expected something more like a James Bond movie set, handsome spies running around with beautiful women and driving sleek sports cars.

Gloria, in a bright floral dress, greeted me at the door and escorted me to a room where my picture and thumbprint were taken. I had been uncertain how to dress but decided I had made a good choice

"

because my dress was similar in style to hers. Within moments, I received a badge. After I read and signed a nondisclosure agreement, Gloria took me to an elevator. The elevator panel showed nine upper floors; however, when Gloria scanned her badge, the elevator seemed to go down. The doors opened to two armed Marines whose faces looked like fists, with no hint of warmth. They asked to see my badge and scanned it with an obscure handheld object. After the check, their expression softened, and they welcomed me as I entered the hallway.

"You'll get used to them," said Gloria.

"I'm curious about the elevator," I said. "I noticed the buttons are for ascending floors, but we went down. Like fourteen floors?"

She smiled. "You're good. Welcome to Neptune, our home away from home."

THIRTY TRIAL DAYS

The first day, I met Lieutenant Thomas Michaels, personal assistant to the assistant director of covert operations (ADCO). He informed me that he would be my interviewer. He was thirtyish, well-groomed, and had a welcoming Southern accent. I noticed he was wearing a wedding band.

He offered me a cup of coffee. I accepted and said, "Thank you, sir." He explained that they weren't that formal underground and to call him Tom. But that when it came time to meet the boss, ADCO General Lang, I was to stand at attention and address *him* as "sir."

The army officer delved right into my life's history. I sat across from him in a bland room: off-white concrete walls, fluorescent lighting, plain tile floor. The whole underground thing was hard to comprehend and a bit claustrophobic. Early into the discussion, I could tell Tom had all the answers. Every place I had ever lived, every school I had attended, the names of my college boyfriends, incidents with my mom, and he even made reference to my ancestral lineage dating back to France.

We took a short break then returned to our seats. By this point in the interview, I had visualized a large window on the wall—a scene of the sea with lots of sunshine. Tom brought out a clipboard and started the questioning.

"Describe how your grandmother Sadie communicated to you after her death: was it by thought, in a vision, or in a dream?

"When you said you've had a reoccurrence of lights flickering on and off, where were you and how often did this happen?

"How'd your lost puppy tell you where to find her?

"How'd you know ahead of time that your mother would push you down the stairs?

"When did you first recall hearing celestial voices?"

After each answer, he made a checkmark on a sheet in front of him. I guessed he was taking my responses and placing them to the appropriate category: clairaudient, clairvoyant, clairsentience, claircognizance, electromagnetic field, mediumship, remote viewing. I assumed a formal assessment of these subjects would come later.

When the interview ended, Gloria was called in. She took me to her office, which was a refreshing departure from everything else I had seen at Neptune. It was like an oasis in the middle of the desert— warm, colorful, friendly, and welcoming. In one corner, a large ball-shaped candle hung from a macramé holder. Although her desk was standard army issue, the accoutrements were things I would've chosen myself—a third eye figurine, a "Tree of Life" painting, a desk lamp with stars and moons that hung about the circumference of the shade. Even her office chair was inspirational with hand-carved birds over each shoulder.

Gloria gave me army-green fatigues with R. Casallie on the shirt pocket. "For the next four weeks you'll answer to the name Rose

Casallie; you're a covert soldier, not a civilian. If you make the grade, you can remain Special Agent Rose Casallie or go home as civilian Sally Stone."

"Why do I need two identities?" I asked. I wanted to ask how long I would be wearing the fatigues. They weren't exactly my color or style, and obviously far from Gloria's wardrobe.

"This isn't a desk job like a secretary or a psychiatrist. Nor is it an FBI position where you would be Agent Sally Stone. This is undercover, where you need to have an assumed identity."

I liked my new name, although I had never heard of Casallie. It sounded close to Joan of Arc's nickname, Pucelle.

"At times, you'll work out in the field with our agents. You'll be traveling. Passports, car rentals, hotels—all will be under your new name. Once you're officially on board, you'll take an oath and learn more about how our department works."

THE SECOND DAY, I took a short helicopter ride to Camp Peary, commonly known as The Farm. My purpose was to observe and learn the terrain before the intense training. I had an ID that said I was a CIA operative. When I entered a big, bowl-like room called the Soup, with wall-to-wall screens and live satellite feeds from around the world, it felt like I was in a science fiction movie. I imagined agents in far-off lands, hustling about under cover of night, meeting in dark alleys, men in black clothes like cat burglars, scaling walls of secluded embassies.

THE FIRST WEEK, I joined ten recruits at the farm. All were CIA except me, who was pretending to be CIA. Each morning, the drill instructor would flip on the lights between 0400 and 0500 and bang our bunks with his nightstick as he rapidly sang a short nursery rhyme. "Mary has a little lamb whose fleece is white as snow," then he would shout, "What color is the lamb?" A new verse each day. "Hey diddle diddle, the cat and the fiddle. Who jumped over the moon?" It was a mental exercise to teach us to think critically the moment we woke up.

NSA's philosophy was that a sharp mind and a strong body work together. The physical exercise began with a five-mile run or walk followed by a combination of calisthenics, isometrics, lifting; sometimes an obstacle course or crawling on our bellies under a web of barbed wire, finishing with more running. The rigorous workout complemented my natural athletic ability.

The second week, mental tests were conducted at the Naval Air Warfare Center in Orlando. I was educated, then quizzed on history, psychology, political science, and geography. Directly after reading thirty-page scenarios and being tested, I learned of countries that I hadn't known existed.

In the third week, I returned to The Farm for more of the same routine.

The fourth week was arms training. This was my least favorite instruction, considering I had never owned or shot a gun before. I knew to stay away from them. I had seen up close what a gun could do in a crazy person's hand.

We learned to break down and assemble multiple different weapons. After static and active target training, we advanced to real-world scenario training. Targets would pop up from all directions. Sometimes an armed assailant, sometimes a nun. We had less than a second to decide to shoot or not. If I shot too soon, the civilian died. If I waited too long, I died.

On the last day of testing, I went to the PX to get my mail and an envelope from Los Angeles stood out. The return address was Aaron Spelling Productions. I could barely open the letter; my hands were shaking as if I had drunk a pot of coffee. I read it and called Gloria.

"It's Rose. You said to call you if I needed anything. Well, I do. I got the part! One of Charlie's Angels. They sent a contract and a time clause. The filming starts in two months. I have to tell them something. I don't know what to do."

"Congratulations. I knew you'd receive interesting offers. You have a paradox; you have two opportunities that could change and shape your life. Both with the same themes, except one is make-believe on television for the whole world to see, and the other is real life, affects real people, and almost no one ever sees."

"Yes, I feel both lucky and uncertain."

"You can make a difference. I was told the same words eleven years ago when I needed to decide between two good options."

According to Gloria, most people at the agency had given up a lucrative or exciting career before signing on. She had been a singer who walked away from a three-album contract with CBS Records. Guaranteed upfront money, six figures. She had been tempted but had no regrets.

"I can share more with you, but I can't make that decision for you. I can impart some of my experiences that may help you see what we are to the program."

"That'd be very helpful. Thank you."

"Meet me tomorrow, 1300 hours in David Houseman's office, and we'll talk."

Four Dead in Ohio

BEFORE MY FEET TOUCHED THE FLOOR, I SCRIBBLED A FEW WORDS in my dream journal.

June 25, 1975. Working at a craft festival, hot and muggy, a very short foreign man, maybe European, was flirting and coming on to me. Dark, crow-like energy around him. Had a gunslinger's gait. When I wasn't looking, he turned into an old woman who bought one of my paintings. It was an interesting dream, but I knew few foreigners and I didn't paint. Well, walls. I knew the value of dreams, especially the warning and prophetic ones. And sometimes a dream was just a dream.

I ARRIVED FIVE MINUTES early at the office called DOS, Director of Spooks. The sign on the door read, *"Anxiety happens when you think you have to figure out everything all at once. Relax, take a breath. We got this, one day at a time."*

Gloria, punctual and upbeat, pulled some papers from her leather briefcase.

"We received several of your assessment results. Anthony Grogan said my insights about you were dead-on, and you gained his approval. Anthony is one of our leading intelligence analyst officers. The first day he met you, he recognized your brightness and was eager to test you. Your IQ score was 127."

"What does that mean?"

"You're in the top twenty percent in the world. Keep in mind, no matter what the scores are, it's the ADCO that makes the final decision." Just hearing the acronym ADCO made me nervous. There were no guarantees the general would even want me.

"I know you were startled to learn that we carry guns. You ranked as an expert marksman on the sidearm qualification test."

"Me, a marksman! I saw I was hitting the targets, but I had no idea how well."

"Your psychic ability enables you to sense and see the target in your mind, not just with your eyes."

"Gloria, have you ever had to use a gun?"

"No. On a lighter note, how do you know so much about astrology? Your scores and written character critiques were impressive. There's no record in the dossier of you studying with a professional."

"My grandmother's sister, Anna Bess, a closet astrologer, started my interest. Every chance she could, she'd tell me things." I thought about the times we had cuddled in her old quilts while staring at the constellations. After we studied our charts, we would analyze other family members. She called it a crazy puzzle. Anna Bess had died the year I left for college. She said I'd go on to do meaningful things.

"It's obvious you had a strong mentor. Astrology is an unexplored resource for us, but we're beginning to look into it more. I find the stars fascinating. I hope we can discuss it more fully in the future."

Gloria shifted the conversation back to the real reason she wanted to meet with me, to illustrate the importance of our role as a psychic and how much David, and the agency, respected and valued our abilities. I listened as I looked at the pictures on the desk. Some were from presidents and prominent dignitaries, with handwritten inscriptions.

She described a scene from 1970 when thousands of college kids had descended on DC to protest the Vietnam War and the Kent State shooting that had taken four student lives. The most deplorable event in US military history, she said. Gloria's job as a lead psychic was to deploy the agency's resources in the best way possible. The goal had been to determine if the protest was a spontaneous student occurrence, or if organized, who had organized and funded it. Before the protest, Gloria had gotten a strong psychic hit.

"I sensed there might be danger at the Lincoln Memorial, even death. I decided to send our newest up-and-coming operative, Robert Sexton."

"Have I met him?" The name sounded familiar. "I overheard his name at lunch yesterday, if it's the same Robert. Two secretaries were comparing notes."

"I'm sure you would've remembered if you had met him. Good-looking. Flirtatious. Wears a Yankees shirt, a lot."

Everyone I had seen at Meade wore either a uniform, jacket and tie, or dress clothes. Before I could ask Gloria about the dress code requirements, she raised her eyebrows and said, "If you come on board, I'll give you the lowdown on Robert. A friendly forewarning of sorts.

"I knew Robert was the agent to send because he'd fit into the crowd with his long, sun-bleached hair and beard. For this assignment, he dressed in patched jeans, a tie-dyed tee shirt, and a blue headband made of a rolled-up kerchief. Nothing happened throughout the day or evening, but in the early morning before daylight, 4:21 a.m. to be exact, President Nixon arrived at the Lincoln Memorial. Without security."

My inquisitive look must have prompted Gloria.

"We don't know. He was upset that American troops had killed American citizens on his watch. He told the protesters he couldn't sleep and wanted to talk to them.

"Robert was in the crowd and stayed close to the president. He noticed a male, early twenties, dressed in a long, heavy coat when one wasn't needed. Robert later described the man as sweating and nervous, and shouldering through the crowd, much like you'd do on a crowded dance floor to get to the other side of the club. The man headed straight for Nixon, and Robert knew the man was going to shoot or stab him. He also thought Secret Service was too far back to intercept the assailant."

I was enthralled by the story when David Houseman came in and turned to Gloria, "Sorry I'm late. Is that the Lincoln Memorial encounter you're talking about?" He apparently seemed interested, sat down behind his desk and told Gloria to continue.

"Robert stepped in between the would-be attacker and Nixon. He spotted a man with a camera in the crowd and asked the president if he could get a picture with him. Nixon agreed. With his arm around him, Robert created a barrier between the president and the assailant. According to the debriefing notes, within seconds four Secret Service agents arrived and one of them grabbed Robert. He looked straight into the agent's eyes then whipped his head around to stare directly at the attacker. The agent understood Robert's body language and seized the man. They took both of them into custody."

Puzzled, I said, "Robert, too?"

"Yes. The good news was that Robert had prevented what could've been a death. The man carried an eight-inch hunting knife. Both he and Robert were interrogated, separately. The bad news was they didn't believe Robert's story—college kid who sensed the danger and reacted. The interrogations continued for two days. They thought Robert had been part of an assassination plot and chickened out at the last minute."

"Why didn't he tell them he was working undercover?"

"We only exist to the president and the DCO. Robert spent his time cuffed to a table, keeping perfectly still, no food, no water, no breaks, no sleep, and forced to wear headphones with loud music. All he admitted was his name, that he went to NYU, and he did not know the assailant. He just knew the man was dangerous. On the second day, he was released."

"Who got him out?"

"I can't share that information with you now. I can tell you that our agents bear a get-out-of-jail card on American soil. In Robert's case, it took forty-eight hours."

"Why that long?"

Gloria looked at David and asked if he wanted to handle that question. David explained that the wheels of bureaucracy turn slowly, almost all the time. Agents are trained to be patient and stay the course. I could tell by the way he spoke about Robert that he held him in high regard.

Gloria continued. "The scene was barely mentioned in the paper. But Robert's actions didn't go unnoticed. After he had had time to recover from the psychological interrogation, the commander-in-chief met with him, learned his real name, and requested his attendance for future settings. A president will remember who you are when you save his life."

David rocked back in his chair, and his eyes seem to glaze over as if he were in deep thought. Then he and Gloria exchanged a few words about Robert. As I listened to them talk about his physical and psychic abilities, I found myself profoundly intrigued by the agency and even more so with Agent Robert Sexton.

They stopped their sidebar and Gloria addressed me. "Rose, one of several scenarios possibly happened that day: maybe Robert had an intervening guardian angel or the president had one, or perhaps a psychic placed the right agent at the right place at the right time."

David nodded and acknowledge Gloria's assessment. Then he

excused himself and said he had a previous appointment and would talk to Gloria later.

Gloria rose from her chair, so I stood also. She looked directly in my eyes. "Rose, this is what we do, but we don't have a script. We're a family here. Relatively small, fifty covert agents and four psychics. We recruit the best and are trained by the best. We work together and sometimes save lives. I know David very well; he wouldn't have participated and stayed as long as he did if he wasn't genuinely hoping you will choose the agency that has chosen you.

"If you become part of our family, I can share more with you. However, no one will think any less of you if you go Hollywood."

I Want to Hold Your Hand

ROBERT HEADED DOWN THE HALL FROM THE OPPOSITE DIRECTION.
There may have been other people in the hallway; I remember him.
I knew it was Robert, and not because of his shirt. I just knew. As I
saw him come closer, I was suspended in some mystical space other
than the brightly lit, sterile hallway. Two strangers approached each
other, closer and closer, and I heard Pavarotti in my head singing "If
We Were in Love." I tried to look away from him and focus on
finding the right room. Instead, I watched his piercing eyes gaze into
my soul, or possibly at my chest. Of all the days to be wearing my
loose-fitting linen dress. At least it was a flattering shade of blue.
Before I knew it, we had arrived at the same door at the same time.
Room 151, the office of Dr. Martin Head, Director of Psychiatry.

"Whoa, who're you?"

"Rose Casallie." I almost said Sally Stone, but I caught myself.

He repeated my name and his body slightly swayed to the words.
"Rose Ca-sal-lie. I'm Robert, Robert Sex-ton."

He lingered on the word, Sex … ton. Or I imagined he did.

"You're the new psychic, the Kentucky girl that turned down
Hollywood for all this luxury."

I tilted my head. "How did you know that?"

"It's not every day we have an angel come on board. Lots of

warriors, Suits, and docs, but few angels. It didn't take long for news of your arrival to float through the ranks."

Amused, I smiled. "I'm not an angel, I just talk to them."

"Interesting."

"Why interesting?"

"Someone who looks like you but is no angel." He stood taller and nodded. "I understand about having to make a hard decision. I had one, too." He pointed to the word *Yankees* on his jersey. I kept looking directly into his hazel eyes. If I looked at his chest, his shoulders, small waist, and tight Levi's, I would lose my already waning composure.

"You're here to see the doc, too? He's known for running late; it's a French thing." He glanced at his watch, a sleek Movado. "Eleven, eleven, my lucky sign. What about we leave a note and grab a cup of coffee? I don't have much time, but I don't want to miss this opportunity to spend more time with you, the angel who is not."

I was willing to forgo the appointment, when the doctor arrived and greeted us both. "Ooh, la la. I had a feeling you two might meet on my watch. How do you say *heureux hasard* …serendipity?" Dr. Head, fast-moving and energetic, waved his hand toward the sofa. "Rose, have a seat. I'll only be a few minutes with Robert."

I sat down in the waiting room and picked up a copy of *Psychology Today*. I couldn't concentrate on the magazine because I was imagining Robert's lips on my cheek, his tight embrace … The door opened and I snapped back to reality. Robert walked out and Dr. Head motioned for me to come into his office. He had read my base evaluations and wanted to discuss them with me. As I stood, Robert came over and held out his hands to mine, palms up. I instinctively put my hands over his. He gazed into my eyes and leaned in.

"Rose, please say it won't be too long before I can hold these hands again." His voice was deep, raspy, and enticing.

I trembled and my heart felt like it was going to leap out of my chest. I half-smiled and pretended to be composed and unaffected by his touch and presence. I needed to focus. Work was why I was here, not romance. Still, I hoped Robert was right that it wouldn't be long before he held my hands again. I sensed it might be a long time. And I sensed I needed to talk to Gloria.

Staying Alive

NOVEMBER 4, 1975

On a solo secret mission, Robert flew to Berlin by Air Force jet. He was briefed in-flight and given a crude satellite photo of the target. His assignment was to recover microfilm that a scientist had hidden in an office at Humboldt University in East Berlin. He didn't and wouldn't know what was in the film. The most difficult part of the assignment was entering and exiting East Germany. Soldiers guarded the borders, equipped with Dragunov sniper semi-automatic rifles and AK47 assault rifles—arms capable of firing ten rounds per second.

Robert, if caught and arrested, would be regarded as a mercenary, willing to sell his goods to the highest bidder. If needed, he had cyanide capsules to take his own life to avoid being tortured. Nothing could connect him to the NSA, CIA, or the US.

No weapons were allowed through the checkpoints. Before departure, Robert's handler gave him a special pen and instructions on how to use it. The pen's fine point became a needle, releasing poison when clicked. A quiet death followed in less than ten seconds.

Fake credentials, visa, and college ID that said he was a postgraduate student got him across the border. Robert located the pre-arranged cab.

"People who need people," Robert said.

"Are the luckiest people in the world," the cab driver said.

"Barbara."

"Streisand."

The cab dropped Robert off at the university and he found the applied science building, Setron Gebäude. Robert surveyed the landscape for signs of danger and suspicious activity. He spotted a small KGB agent named Vladimir Putin, whom he'd met a year earlier in Helsinki. This seemed strange, so he made a mental note of the agent's exact location then continued.

The security guard frisked and wanded Robert as he entered the building. He cleared security and located Room 208. The door was unlocked, and the microfilm was where it was supposed to be, flat and taped to the bottom of the second drawer on the desk's right side. Robert placed the microfilm in an envelope and slipped it in his shirt pocket just as a man dressed in civilian clothes entered the room.

The man, robust, six-foot-four, and fortyish, held his hand out and demanded that Robert, who was cornered behind the desk, give him the envelope. Robert assumed the man was not carrying a gun, as he hadn't pulled one out. Robert sized up the situation in seconds. The man seemed overconfident because of his physique and age, and Robert decided to use that against him.

The man pulled a knife from his jacket and lunged across the desk. Robert grabbed a book lying on the desk and whacked the man across the forehead while he blocked his hand brandishing the knife. The assailant, breathing heavily and reeling from the blow to his head, backed off momentarily.

"We don't have to do this," Robert said. "You can go home. You look like you have a family. Look into my eyes: I'm leaving here with the film. You can't stop me. I'll take you out if you make another move. Let's just both go home. You tell your people the film was already gone."

"I cannot do that. I must be victorious," said the German in his broken Eastern European English.

"You will not win. Go back to your family."

Without warning, the German attacked again. Robert sidestepped and hit him squarely in the throat with his fist. The man gasped for air and stood straight. Robert jumped on the desktop and pulled out his pen.

Robert firmly stated, "You would be wise to go now. I will kill you if you do not leave." His opponent moved toward him. Robert deployed the special pen and stabbed the German between neck and shoulder. After a few seconds, the man collapsed. Robert dragged the motionless body to a closet. He knew he had just killed a KGB agent. He looked at his watch, wiped down everything he had touched, ditched his book bag, and headed for the East Berlin border.

Leaving East Germany proved more difficult than entering. The stamp in Robert's passport showed that he'd just arrived. The guard asked him why he was leaving so soon. Robert said he had left his book bag filled with important school papers at the airport and had to retrieve them. He hoped that his hippie-like looks would be convincing, and his exit timely before the corpse was discovered.

When he returned to the US Army base in Berlin, Robert received a phone call from ADCO Lang, congratulating him for retrieving the microfilm. Robert felt conflicted about receiving accolades, considering he had killed a man to get the job done. General Lang told him he needed to go directly to Budapest.

If You Could Read My Mind

Robert was in no mood to banter back and forth with a shrink. He had a disdain for the entire psychological evaluation process but knew he had to comply with Dr. Head's directives or be benched. It wasn't his first kill, nor his first time being combative with Dr. Michelle Thompkins.

"Well, Robert, here we are again. From the report, you must have a lot going on in your head. I'm here to assist you the best I can. Would you like a cup of tea? I have Earl Grey."

Robert shook his head. "No."

"So tell me what happened."

Before answering, Robert swung one of the steel balls in the Newton's cradle on Dr. Thompkins's desk. He leaned back in his chair, crossed his arms, and stared at the cradle as he spoke. "You know what went down. You read the briefings."

"Yes, but I would like to hear it in your own words. It may help to talk about it and deal with your emotions. After all, you did kill a man. That bothered you enough to influence your next assignment."

Dr. Thompkins added a touch of cream and honey to her freshly brewed tea, sipped it, and tried to get Robert to talk about the Budapest assignment. Robert's debriefing had explained that the mission had been to extract Ivan Viktor, a former double agent and now a Russian defector. Unfortunately, he had been captured by his own people and was about to be extradited to Moscow for trial, a pretense for his execution. An undercover agent had been in touch with him. US operatives were to snatch him when he was escorted from the local jail and fly him to Switzerland. It was supposed to look like the work of renegade Russian dissidents. Robert's job was simple: kill Viktor if he tried to double-cross or make a run for it. If the KGB was successful in extraditing Viktor, most likely evidence would point to the US's involvement in a Russian state matter, on their soil, behind the Iron Curtain.

Robert had had him in his gun sights when Viktor ran, and the lead told him to take the target down. There were several people nearby and Robert hesitated less than a second, but that was enough for Viktor to board and take control of a school bus that had stopped nearby. The local authorities gave chase while Robert's unit scrambled to evacuate. Ground agents later reported that Viktor eventually lost control of the bus and went over a cliff. Everybody on board had died, including eleven children.

Michelle, after hearing Robert's account, refreshed her hot tea, stirred it slightly, and asked, "How does all this make you feel?"

Robert looked up from the hypnotic motion of the swinging balls. "Really! That's all you got? How do I feel? Are you fucking crazy? How would anyone feel if they were responsible for killing eleven children?"

"You're not responsible."

"I'm not? Then why have I had the same nightmare for the last four nights? It was my mistake. Not taking the shot."

Robert described the dream. The eleven kids, along with their parents, appeared around him. The children were lean, their skin pale. They had bobbed haircuts and stoic expressions. The parents' faces were somber and angry. All of the parents and children had a sinister presence; staring endlessly at Robert without moving, they closed in on him from all sides. They were dressed in the bland gray clothing typical of the people of Hungary.

Robert heard voices speaking in broken English with a strong Eastern European accent. "Vhy did you let us die … vhy didn't you help us …vhy didn't you save us …vhy did you let our children die … ve thought Americans good people." He would wake up, go back to sleep, and the dream would start again. Each time a sense of guilt loomed throughout his visions.

"Dreams, even the unsettling ones, are good. They're a way to help us cope with life. Please go on …"

"There's nothing to go on about. I didn't take the shot! But I'll tell you exactly how I feel. This conversation is pointless, plain bullshit. You have no idea what it's like to do what we do. If you did, you wouldn't ask such inane questions."

"Very good, you're angry. Let's go with that."

"We're soldiers, warriors, we do what is needed. We're trained not to think about the crap you're asking about. Listen, when I signed on, I agreed to do whatever it takes to ensure America always comes out on top. You don't get it. War is ugly, it has to be, or there would be more of it."

Dr. Thompkins said in a quiet voice, almost a whisper, "I hear you. We'll move on."

Robert had figured out long ago that Dr. Thompkins had a "tell." Whenever she felt she was in control of the conversation, she would speak softer, almost a little sexier, but not quite. The more she led the discussion, the softer her voice became. It was not obvious to an average person, but Robert was not average. His IQ was 151. And he was trained to notice everything. His life often depended on recognizing the little nuances and idiosyncrasies most would miss.

"Do you want to discuss what happened in East Germany?"

"No, I don't. His choice to die. My choice to live. Michelle, I'm done talking. Now you get in your Beemer, drive to your luxury Georgetown condo, put on Captain and Tennille's "Love Will Keep Us Together" and sip your Sterling cab. This is over for you, I'm the one who has to live with it." Robert rose from his chair, paused for a moment, and flashed his charming smile. "I'm sorry for my language and sarcasm. I don't dismiss what you do here, I know you mean well. I also know you can ground me with a 'Not Fit for Duty.'"

Dr. Thompkins looked into her cup. "I understand the situation you're in. I'm not second-guessing your actions or motives. We'll revisit this in the future. We're both part of this team and have roles to perform. I genuinely care about you. I will finalize my evaluation today."

"Thank you."

Robert went directly to the ADCO's office. Being called to General Lang's office was a bit intimidating for him. After all, he fancied himself as a rock star agent; now he had been summoned like a schoolboy to see the principal. The ADCO's office was the largest on the floor. It was dimly lit except for desk lamps that illuminated the workspace. This made the general seem larger than life.

Robert knocked on the door. General Lang called, "Come on in. At ease, soldier."

On the wall behind the desk were pictures of all the presidents he had served under, from President Johnson to the current president, President Ford. President Nixon's inscription read, "America thanks you for your outstanding service. Respectfully, Richard M. Nixon."

"Son, sometimes in war things don't go as planned. Innocent lives are lost. These things can't be helped. It's not like you're playing God, deciding who lives and who dies. Your training has taught you that civilian lives are paramount to protect. You did that when you chose not to shoot. It was the right decision."

"Permission to speak openly, sir."

"The only way to ever speak. Never pull punches with me. What's on your mind?"

"It bothers me that a psychiatrist gets to say whether or not I am fit for duty."

"You're not dangling on whether she says so." He pointed to his sleeve. "I outrank any psychiatrist."

"Regardless, I'm unsure if I missed the chance at the shot because I was worried about the safety of others, or if I froze because of my most recent kill. Either way, eleven children died."

"Hell, I don't know any shooters that haven't hesitated once or twice. The fact that taking a life is difficult speaks to your character. These deaths are on Viktor, not you. For the record, the lead reports your choice as the correct course of action. There was no shot!

"I read the debriefing on Germany. The man you killed was actually a Russian KGB agent, Alexander Putin. He was a vicious and immoral agent. He has a nephew who is a rising star in the KGB, Vladimir Putin. Keep an eye on him whenever he's around. We think he is following in his uncle's footsteps. I concur with the lead; you followed the rules of engagement. I'm proud to have you as a key member of our defense team. Now carry on, soldier. Dismissed!"

Robert left the general, and before leaving for furlough, he headed over to the Spooks department in hopes of finding Rose Casallie. He wasn't sure why. David informed him that Rose was out of the office and on assignment with Gloria.

Scandal

 in Winter Park. As he drove up the long, winding, thickly wooded driveway, he was uncharacteristically thinking about staying in for the night. Usually he was more than ready to regain his identity. Winston Forester. Musician. The more distractions, the better, and less time to think about what his alter ego had been through. That was his way to cope—music, movies, fast cars, and pretty girls. Play music in the nightclubs, attract the babes, have sex, and do it all over the next day and night.

His housekeeper had left at six o'clock that evening and had already fed the dogs. Two beautiful golden retrievers ran out of the house to greet their friend and master. He checked the mail that had been left for him on the kitchen table. With several packages left to open, he looked in the refrigerator and found a fresh meatloaf sandwich waiting for him, lettuce on the side as usual. He put it together, added a healthy amount of ketchup, and his dinner was ready.

Before he showered, he went outside to commune with the many birds in the bird aviary. It was a four hundred square foot environment that housed more than fifty birds, complete with heat for the winter and small trees and shrubs. Although it had perimeter feeders, when Robert was home he fed and watered the birds himself.

After a brief visit in the aviary, he bathed, and then headed to the couch to finish reading a book that a close friend had sent him, *All the President's Men.* He was eager to read it, because he knew all the players. He also knew that only he and his associates understood what had really taken place with Watergate. If Nixon had wanted to bug the Democratic National Committee, he would've simply ordered the NSA to conduct the surveillance, invoking the presidential privilege.

If Robert had been twenty years older, President Nixon might have listened to him instead of the White House chief of staff. The Suits at the White House saw Robert as only a "seen but not heard" asset. Bob Haldeman was the one who informed Nixon about the break-in. Unfortunately, the president had made a fatal mistake by not calling the FBI as soon as he was aware of the situation. Instead, he chose to be part of the cover-up.

Robert was disenchanted with the book and the whole affair. He reflected on Nixon's choices: Here was a man who had won re-election by an amazing landslide, the biggest, most overpowering victory in American history; he had stopped a war, retrieved POWs from Vietnam, ended the draft, created a school meal program for disadvantaged children, lowered the voting age, desegregated American schools, initiated the Clean Air and Clean Water Acts, signed the first weapons treaty with Russia to limit strategic arms, and been the first president to visit China. Yet because he chose to participate in the cover-up, he would be remembered for that incident rather than for his accomplishments. Watergate proved an axiom that Robert learned in grade school, absolute power corrupts absolutely.

Robert mused about what would happen if the public were to find out that six presidents had used his division, Covert Operations, on their watch. Now *that* would be a bestseller and a blockbuster, and maybe the biggest scandal in US history. *All the President's Real Men.*

Actually, Robert remembered that it was only five presidents and not six. DCO General Stevens had made a decision to keep President Ford in the dark about their department. Ford was the only president or vice-president never elected to the office—he had been appointed vice president following the resignation of Spiro Agnew and became president when Nixon resigned. General Stevens believed that President Ford would be a short-term president and he didn't need to know about Covert Operations.

After Robert finished the book, he realized it was ten o'clock and he was still alone. He thought about Rose. That was indeed strange behavior, to be thinking about a girl other than just for sex.

Robert pulled out his little black book to see who was available. He started with Ginger because she had a sister. He had better odds of a hook-up with two girls living in the same house.

Before he could finish saying hello, Ginger said, "Winston Forester, you think you can disappear for a couple of weeks, no call, no goodbye, then when you show up, I'm supposed to drop everything and go out this late at night?"

"Kind of, I was hoping that your sister would come out too. We could make our own X-rated movie."

"You'd better be joking. It's either me or Julie. Make up your mind!"

It had worked. Robert had hoped bringing up her sister would distract Ginger into letting go of the "Where have you been?" attitude.

Before heading out to meet Ginger, Robert called Cheryl to line up a date for Saturday. She was always glad to see him. No questions asked. No problems.

Double Vision

THE TIME HAD COME. MY FIRST FIELD ASSIGNMENT. A WELCOME change from the previous week's work in which we had read local newspapers from cities all over the world, searching for an intuitive flash that might interest the ADCO. And we had read dozens of threat letters for the same purpose. All behind a desk.

I realized that in less than six months I had gone from Sally Stone, a psychic that talks to angels, to Rose Casallie, a semi-soldier using my clairvoyant skills to aid the government on a reconnaissance team, helping them stay safe while they execute the objectives of their predefined sanctioned missions.

Headed for Birmingham, Alabama, on a Beechcraft Super King, known for its speed, payload, range, and unusually quiet interior, I read the dossier: *Weathermen are an extreme offshoot of the sixties terrorist group, Students for the Democratic Society. The SDS was the organization that fueled the rage on campuses all across America. On May 4, 1970, they held a protest rally on the campus of Kent State. We know how badly that ended. The Weathermen are not students. They are a small group of terrorists that want to bring the United States down.*

In the past year and a half, they have detonated twenty-five bombs. Local, state, and FBI are all working feverishly on collecting as much data as possible on the who, where, and when of the Weathermen's next target. When the group attacked the headquarters of the US State Department, they became a top priority for the DOD. We have credible intel that a Marine recruitment office in Birmingham was targeted by the group. Objective: stop the bombing, catch the bombers.

I understood that on this task I would be assisting Gloria. Her role was to contribute any information that would help our field agent disarm an anticipated bomb. From my training, I knew we have a better than seventy percent accuracy rate. Gloria had an eighty-five percent accuracy quotient.

I thought it was bizarre that a person would kill in the name of peace. A life was a life.

Gloria picked me up at the army aviation support facility north of Birmingham. She opened with, "I love your outfit." I was dressed in high-waisted pleated bellbottom jeans with embroidery on the lower legs, a knit top that accentuated my curves, layers of beaded necklaces, and large sunglasses. She had told me to wear clothes that made me look like a shopper, not a copper. Gloria looked stunning in a tight-fitting maroon pantsuit. The low neckline and strands of pearls would catch any eye.

Our destination was the Marine recruitment headquarters located in a small strip mall on Third Avenue, one mile northwest of the University of Alabama campus. We arrived at 0800. The bomb squad had already secured the area. The shopping plaza had sixteen storefronts. All were closed. No cars or people were within the perimeter of the recruitment office parking lot. We set up our viewing point within a hundred yards in front of the center, with a clear view of the entire strip. Karl, our bomb expert for this mission, was on the grounds about thirty feet from the target. His team had secured the back parking lot as well.

Gloria explained that the *modus operandi* for the previous bombings of recruitment offices had been to attach a small charge directly to the bottom of the front door. There had been two deaths so far. It could've been much more, but most sergeants and staff parked in the rear and entered through the back door. Gloria and I were in position. I felt a flush of emotions: anxious, exhilarated, and scared.

I studied my mentor's movements and wondered how she cleared her head to zone in.

Karl, on his squawk box, said, "Gloria, I'm going dark in thirty seconds. I'm using the back door for access. Any last-minute instructions?"

She closed her eyes for a moment, with a perplexed look, and said, "No instructions but give me a minute." She paused. "I think we're good to go."

"Ten seconds till dark," he replied.

Gloria glanced at me with a deep, poignant stare. I got a vision and blurted out, "NO, NO. NO. Stop! The back door is going to blow up!"

"Karl, do you copy?" Gloria said. "Use the front door!"

"Acknowledged."

"We have you in our sight and in our prayers," Gloria replied.

It took less than a minute for Karl to be repositioned at the front door. *Who am I to override Gloria?* He grabbed the door handle, picked the lock, and turned the knob. *A man could die.* It seemed to take ten minutes for the lock to turn. He opened the door ever so slightly, then swung it open wide.

Back on the box, Karl said, "Gloria, I see the bomb on the back door. Thanks, I'll take it from here."

As we headed back to the airbase, Gloria congratulated me and said I had saved Karl's life and possibly more lives. I asked her why she had deferred to me so quickly. What if I had been wrong?

"I was in charge of the safety of the mission. I tuned in with all my abilities to protect Karl. It was then that I channeled you. I could see your aura. I knew you were in the moment, that you saw things I didn't. My ability wasn't seeing where the bomb was, it was seeing that I knew *you* knew where the bomb was. We're a team."

She went on to clarify that the field agent ultimately, and sometimes within seconds, makes the call to trust a psychic's judgment or not. Some agents request the Spooks more than others. Karl was one of them.

We boarded the plane. Our next flight was to take us to other federal locations for observation and clairvoyant receptions. Once there, our job was to get a sense of the lay of the land, looking for psychic hits or premonitions. The first ten minutes in the air, Gloria was making notes and few words were exchanged. I was still tense from the earlier experience. It seemed surreal.

My thoughts managed to turn to my mother. Gloria was such a contrast to her. My mother rarely honored any opinion that was different from hers, especially my intuitive ones. She had often accused me of being from another planet, or a witch of some sort. The painful memory emerged, the one where my mother said she wished I had never been born. I wondered if she meant it, and why. Part of me wished I could share my new identity and role with my family, primarily to show that my gifts were finally being valued.

I often wondered if my grandmother would still be alive today had my mother listened to me. It wasn't the car accident that had killed Sadie; it was having her hair done in the hospital and the hair spray that was used on her. I had told my mother to not let the nurse do her hair. I had expressed the exact words I had heard: "The fumes will kill her." Mom had ridiculed my spirit friend and ignored the warning. A few hours after her beauty treatment, Sadie had experienced an asthma attack, her lungs had collapsed, and she had died. The memory still bothered me. I had only been ten years old, but it hadn't been my first premonition that came true.

When Gloria put down her pen, my childhood memories receded. "Remember, you were going to give me some forewarnings on Robert Sexton if I came on board? This may be a good time. I finally met him. We arrived at Dr. Head's office at the same moment. I can't get him out of my mind."

"No coincidences. Dr. Head probably planned it, or Robert for that matter. I told you he was easy on the eyes; he can charm any girl and even his bosses. Dress codes are not for him; he can wear his signature Yankees shirt anytime he wants. Dating rule—not to date within the ranks—he breaks it. Well, technically, it may not be called dating if you go out with him."

"How does he get away with it?"

"Because he's the fastest, strongest, smartest operative we have. With that goes the same perks that a star athlete would enjoy. He has enough clout; he can make his own rules." Gloria paused. "Did he swoop you up after laying eyes on you?"

"Almost. We were about to leave but Dr. Head arrived. Before Robert left the office, he came over to say goodbye, and reached for my hands and held them."

"That sounds like him; he likes to touch. He's physical."

"I didn't want to let go."

"Oh, lord, I can tell you have fallen for him by the sound of your voice and that dreamy look on your face. Remember he's popular with all the girls, on and off base. Off base, he's a musician, known to have a different girl every night. He often gets mistaken for Barry Gibb of the Bee Gees." Gloria added with a smirk, "His mama probably told him he was just too pretty for one girl and then sent him to charm school."

I laughed quietly and daydreamed about the pretty, bad boy. I had no trouble visualizing Robert. "Do you know his birthdate?"

"I don't. I think he's a Libra. I can find out."

"If you can, will you try and get the exact time he was born? Libra and Scorpio. Air and water. Not a great fit. But if I had the time, I can do his whole chart and see if we're compatible. When's your birthday, Gloria?"

"I'm a Leo, July twenty-seventh."

I Just Want to Celebrate

WE TRAVELED AROUND THE SOUTH SEVERAL MORE DAYS, VISITING other recruiters. There was nothing as intense or hands-on as my first assignment. On our arrival back at Fort Meade, Gloria debriefed. I went with her.

David said, "I read the report, but Gloria, is there anything you want to add?"

"No, the mission was successful. It was tense for a short time, but when we saw the front door open with no explosion, we knew we had made the right choice. The forensics went in and we took off."

"Well, girls, I have some good news. Because Karl defused the bomb intact, we were able to get a good amount of evidence. We turned it over to the FBI, which led to the arrest of the bombers. It was the work of the Weathermen. With the evidence collected, many terrorists will be going to jail. This may break the back of the group. Without fingerprints, bomb parts, and the type of explosives, the Weathermen would be perpetrating more violent acts. Excellent job, Gloria. Now Rose, please go check the dossier on your desk for your next assignment."

As I walked toward my office, I felt dejected, unappreciated. *Did I misjudge Gloria?* I thought we had connected on another level. That she could be a friend, mentor, even mother figure. It occurred to me that maybe she was my mother in disguise, telling me one thing, doing another, never acknowledging my achievements. I told myself to quit obsessing about my childhood and move on. This mission was about saving lives and not about my hurt feelings when I didn't receive praise. Gloria was the one in charge, and the mission was successful due to her choices. She should get the accolades.

I read the dossier, and to my surprise, it was only one page with an obscure and ominous message: *"Rose Casallie, it's time for you to get on the ball, time to make a difference. Go to Room 142, briefing for your next assignment."*

The dossier said to open the door and take a seat. *Had I made a wrong decision enlisting with the agency?* As I opened the door, I heard voices shouting, "Congratulations Rose! You're one of us." There were balloons and a cake. A wall-to-wall banner read, "We couldn't have done it without you," signed by Karl and the team. David and Gloria were all smiles, and they led with a barrage of hugs. I felt I had arrived, that I had a family.

After about thirty minutes, David congratulated me one more time. He instructed everyone to return to their work before the ADCO got wind of us having fun. The general only half appreciated what our department did. David told everybody to clean up as if the party had never happened. Covert Operations were more hardcore military, unlike the Spooks, who are much more informal and intimate.

My good fortune continued. When I left the room, the pretty, bad boy was outside the door, leaning against the wall.

"Hello, ladies."

Before I spoke, Gloria said, "Well, hello, Robert, what are you doing here, hanging out in the hallway? David told us you were on a twelve-day furlough in Florida."

Robert turned to me. "I flew back to ask Rose for lunch."

Did I hear him correctly? Flew back? Lunch? I froze for a second, glanced at Gloria, and responded, "Sure, I'm done for the day at noon, only a few more notes to write."

"Just the answer I wanted; I'll stop by your office at 1200 hours. Always wonderful to see you, G."

"Likewise."

Robert disappeared like lightning and Gloria turned to me. "I knew he would track you down."

As we were about to part ways I said, "Why did he call you 'G'? Is there something that I don't know about?"

"No, no. When I gave you the scoop on him, I should've told you that at one time we were more than friends. It didn't go anywhere. Don't get me wrong, we're close, I love him like a brother. He gives pet names to his intimate friends. I got 'G'.

"Go enjoy lunch. You two look good together. He has a different look in his eyes when he stares at you. You may be the one that changes the Hawk's reputation."

"Hawk …what did you say?"

"Yes. You know a hawk can spot and strike his prey from any distance. The girls on base gave him that name. Let me know how it goes."

Day Dream

ROBERT SHOWED UP EARLY IN TIGHT JEANS AND A LONG-SLEEVE fitted Beatles tee shirt. "Are you ready to rock, Rosie?"

"Give me a second or two." Rosie, I thought. Now I had a nickname, too. Of all the days to be stuck in my office and in my work clothes. I wish I would have had time to go home and change into my new sleeveless black jumpsuit. Instead, my mid-calf pleated skirt and white button-up blouse would have to do.

"I know this cool little café in Fredrick, about an hour from here. Hope you like salads, that's all they serve. All-natural, vegetarian, and with home-made dressings, freshly made teas, too."

"Sounds terrific, and yes, I love salads."

Of course, any place would be fine with Robert. Since our first meeting, he'd been my on my mind, and my desire. As we approached a shiny blue Corvette Stingray, he opened the passenger door for me.

"Thank you. Love your car."

"Baby, it's you, want to drive? You'd look good behind the wheel. Your baby blues match the color."

I told him no thanks and thought he would never put me in the driver's seat if he knew my driving record. Not to mention that I was under the influence of infatuation.

The trip to the Green Tree Café was more magical than expected. After cruising at high speeds on I-70, Robert veered off the main route. He pulled over and changed what I thought was a hard-top sports car into a convertible. He wanted me to have a clear view of the Utica Covered Bridge we were about to go through. The enchanting old bridge, built in 1831, was certainly worth driving thirteen miles out of the way just to cross. I glanced over at him. I was falling hard.

We arrived at the café and the waiter sat us in a secluded spot surrounded by flowering trees and colorful gardens. Waiting to place our order, I asked him why he was back from furlough so early.

"I flew in to find you. After seeing you at the doc's office, I couldn't wait to stare into those eyes again. But duty called first …"

I wanted to ask him where he'd been, but I was pretty sure that it was improper protocol. NSA. Never Say Anything, even to coworkers.

"I estimated your arrival time back on base and took my chances. Flew in commercially to see if I could catch the angel girl and take her to an intimate lunch. After all, you're without a doubt the hottest girl that's ever been at Fort Meade."

As I soaked up his flattering words, Gloria's remarks kept replaying in my head. A different girl every night, on and off base.

My cheeks heated up and I couldn't keep silent. "I guess I should say thank you for the compliment since rumor has it you're acquainted with the majority of the girls on base rather intimately, including my mentor, Gloria. I mean your G."

"Awe, what did G tell you? That was early on; she's too old for me …"

"Just a warning of sorts. Don't worry; G is still a big fan of yours. Oh, she did mention that you like playing by your own rules. Like ignoring no dating within the ranks."

"Guilty as charged."

He smoothly changed the subject and congratulated me on my first field assignment and party. He cocked his head slightly and asked, "Can a psychic be surprised at her own surprise party?"

"Well, I guess so, I was. They set me up well. I didn't see it coming." This might have been the time to share that the accuracy rate deteriorates rapidly for a psychic when it pertains to personal matters. It's much easier to be accurate when you're objective and hold no emotional attachment to the outcome, particularly with affairs of the heart. I held back though; he probably already understood that.

A waitress came over and asked if we were ready to order. It seemed like she knew Robert by the tone of her voice, but that may have just been in my head. Robert asked her to give us a few minutes. She was quite attractive. I noticed that he hardly looked at her and kept his eyes on me.

Curious, I asked, "How were you recruited?"

"I had been on their radar for a long time …. I was at the beach, Long Beach, south shore Long Island where I grew up. Seventeen. Been out surfing, came in …" My attention briefly strayed as I imagined him surfing on the waves …no shirt, exposed chest, toned muscles, golden tan …the theme of *Jaws* in the background …. "Stuck my board in the sand and laid on the blanket when two guys approached me in suits."

The image of men in suits on the beach snapped me back to attention. He continued. "These guys said I needed to come with them. I told them they were crazy as hell. They pulled their jackets back and showed me that they had guns. I said, 'Unless you show me a badge, I'm still not going with you. If you were going to shoot me, you would've already done it.' One of them pulled out a federal marshal's badge and said, 'Your Uncle Winston wants to talk to you, and he said you might be a smart ass.' They pointed in the direction of a giant black Cadillac limo.

"I laughed and walked over, and my uncle rolled down the window and said, 'Winston, come for a ride. It's time we talk; it's time for you to learn about our lineage."

Before I could ask who Winston was, Robert said, "Breaking another rule, Rosie, my name is Winston Forester."

"Sounds so regal, English." I love that he had shared this with me.

"The Foresters' dedication to service is documented back as far as twelve hundred AD. We have served kings, prime ministers, presidents. Winston Forester was the bodyguard for King Henry III."

"Are you named after him?"

"I'm named after my great Uncle Winston, the one in the limo. He was a founding member of the CIA, the NSA, and the DIA."

"Wow, impressive. What's the DIA?"

"Defense Intelligence Agency, the specialist branch that interrogates prisoners."

"I don't know about that."

"Well, you're not supposed too, it is as-needed-only basis."

Robert continued to talk proudly and passionately about his ancestry. "My other uncle, Uncle Jack, Winston's brother, was far more flamboyant about his dedication to service. He was a pilot in WWI, the only pilot to fly for two countries concurrently. He flew for England and the US, and was decorated by King George V and President Woodrow Wilson. After the war, he rode with the Texas Rangers and occasionally went undercover and rode with the Mexican Diablo gang. He was also one of the original pilots for US Air Mail. On the edge of everything. That's what I mean when I say I've been on their radar for a long time. It's in our genes."

"I guess so." Jeans … he filled them out well.

"My uncle told me he'd been watching me since I was born. He knew stories about me. And because of what he knew, he said: You're one of us.

"He told me about the NSA, how long it had been around, and that they had created a new experimental division within the agency, a covert division, and they needed someone like me. He made me out like I was a bionic man. 'Athletic, strong, smart, sixth sense, fearless … you know what to do when you don't know what to do.' With a deadpan face and a sharp tone, he said, 'You don't have to join us, but if you don't, I'll have to kill you.'"

"Kill you?"

"For a split-second, I thought he was serious until he smiled and hugged me. He went on to say, 'Winston, you can choose any career you want … baseball player, musician. I know you want to play for the Yankees, everyone in your family knows it. You may be one of the fastest kids in the country, all the scouts realize it.'"

"Oh, I got it now, your jersey. I thought you were just a fan! You could've been one."

Robert continued with his uncle's recruitment tactics. "'A life of service could be the best life you could ever have, but you'll never be a Yankee or a millionaire.' And he ended with his often-plagiarized quote … 'You can make money, or you can make a difference.'"

"Yes, yes, I've heard it; Anthony and Gloria used that on me too."

He laughed. "I think it must be in their recruiting manual. The line seems to work. After all, I'm in the company with what could have been one of *Charlie's Angels* …"

I blushed. Robert finished the story. "Well, the limo dropped me off at my house. I was amazed to find both my surfboard and car in the garage. That's when I realized they could do anything. My keys were still in my pocket. It was a lot to think about, and a lot to walk away from, but pretty exciting. Trade a baseball career for a chance to be 007 and continue in the tradition of the Foresters. And now because of my choice, and your choice, I'm sitting here with Winston's Angel … Sally Stone."

"Sally Stone! Did you say … How …"

"Yeah, I have my ways of finding out things. I had some time off in Florida after a few assignments; I was daydreaming about you …"

He had been thinking about me … the bad boy rumored to have a different girl every night …

"Yes, musing about the new angel girl." He held out his hands, palms up, like at our first encounter. I laid mine on top. "I did a little digging around and retrieved a copy of that angel show you were on. Learned about Sally Olivia Stone, angels, and musicians who have angels. Don't worry; I'll keep your name a secret. I'll keep calling you Rose, to abide by the rules. Is that okay, Rosie?" He winked and gave my hands a soft squeeze, and we gently let go.

On the drive back, the song "Mustang Sally" came on the radio. He started singing … "Ride Sally Ride," glanced at me, and said, "I have a story about the making of that song. Maybe I'll save that for dinner tomorrow."

He had found a smooth way of asking me out again, without asking. And I accepted the dinner invitation by not saying anything. I wondered if I was out of my league with him. On the drive home— radio playing, top-down—I tried to imagine where this was going. By the end, I had convinced myself, love and romance would be the perfect antidotes for such an intense business like the one we were in, regardless of the rules.

When we arrived at my cottage, Robert walked me to the door. He kissed me on the cheek to say goodbye, and as he turned to leave, he came back and gave me another kiss on the lips. I returned his kiss with a deep, passionate kiss of my own, one that said I wanted more.

Mustang Sally

I HARDLY SLEPT THAT NIGHT. THE NEXT DAY FLEW BY. EARLY THAT evening, there was a knock at the door. It was Robert. He entered with, "Hey babe, I got pizza, music, and time for us."

I liked the sound of "Hey babe." This time I had on my jumpsuit. I wasn't sure what he would think of my decorating skills. All of the cottages were identical in size and color. To be creative, I had painted all my ceilings and walls in a soft shade of blue, replaced the Venetian blinds with fabric and lace, and set a few crystals in the entrance.

"You look awesome in that outfit, and you have a very cool space. I also have beads hanging in my doorways, back in Winter Park. Maybe you can come to visit sometime." Robert raised his eyebrows. "I also have a heated waterbed." I didn't respond, just pictured the scene in my mind.

I remembered from lunch that he liked half-sweet tea; I had some already brewed and poured him a glass. By the time I served it, he had Bruce Springsteen's new album, *Born to Run,* on the record player. I grabbed some plates and napkins and we ate our pizza on the outside deck.

"Thinking about what you said yesterday— the thing about being a New York Yankee—you must have been in great form before you were trained."

"My dad instilled in me that if you're going to do something, do it the best you can or don't do it. He taught me many things, and one was to be physically fit. My goal was to be the best centerfielder for the best team in the world. When I took a different path, I decided I was going to be the best undercover agent in the world. I'm trying to do that. I've been lucky to have had great mentors, and now lucky to be here with you."

"Thank you." I felt my face turning red. I shifted the focus away from me. "What were your parents like growing up?"

"Well, my dad was like *Father Knows Best*, Howard Cunningham, and Charlton Heston in *The Ten Commandments* all rolled into one."

"And your mother?"

"She would be a mix of Mrs. C, Eleanor Roosevelt, and Dinah Shore. Everyone called her Mom; she always had food for everybody. She knitted sweaters, made homemade pastries and cakes, and was a church youth group leader. She constantly sang songs. My parents were just here for a visit. I took them to Disney World."

I thought, *This guy can't be for real, and for sure the parents can't be. His mom sings in the house. They go to Disney World together.* I decided it was best to leave my family out of the *Happy Days* conversation and focus on him. After all, I wanted another date. After hearing about his family, I imagined he had family photos everywhere in his home. I became self-conscious that my walls only had photos of my beloved four-leggers.

Robert gave credit to others in his life as well as his parents. One was his PE teacher, Mr. Fleckner, a former head coach of the US Olympic gymnastics team who was his instructor from kindergarten through high school.

"He had us running by the age of five, by third grade he had us holding bricks when we ran, and by my senior year, me and a classmate of mine, Julius Irving, had the highest scores in the country on the JFK Physical Fitness test. Dr. J is big now and that's why everyone thought I'd be a professional athlete like him. Instead, I succumbed to the allure of the spy game."

I had no idea what Julius looked like, but I could attest that Robert's physique exhibited exceptional shape. I guessed he had a forty-two-inch chest and a twenty-seven-inch waist, weighed about a hundred and sixty-five pounds, and had rock hard muscles. I had to remind myself to focus on his words, not his body, or his face. If his classmates only knew about his profession now. I asked, "Did your training intensify when you became an agent?"

"Yeah, I've been trained by the best doctors, scientists, and teachers. My instruction was worth millions of dollars. Trained in self-defense, we learned how to destroy, kill, and hurt; how to break bones; how to inflict enough pain to get information, mostly when and where to use those skills. Drilled to run five miles wearing a thirty-pound lead vest. Coached to do a four-foot vertical jump with a full backpack and weapons in both hands."

"How many of you were trained like that?"

"Only a handful. They took our natural abilities and honed them to a level of invincibility, at least that's what I felt. And Rosie, you'll get to be the best in your expertise, too, but you might not need training. I suspect that you're a natural-born psychic."

"I suppose I am. Psychic sensitivity runs in my family. It has skipped generations, and there's a tale, maybe a tall tale, that my ancestry goes back to the family of Joan of Arc. I'd like to think I'm related to a saint, whether it's true or not."

Showing off his knowledge of French, Robert said, "Jehanne d'Arc of Domrémy. Saint and warrior. Cool lineage if true."

When I got up to get him some more tea, he stood, grabbed my right hand, and turned me toward him. "Your eyes are captivating, but your body is hot." He picked me up off the floor as he kissed me in a way I've only seen in movies. I was caught off guard and couldn't remember what I was doing. I thought it was best to get the tea.

Gray clouds and a few drops of rain were moving in on us. It was good timing to relocate into the living room. I might have jumped his body and torn off his shirt right there on the deck.

Being so close to Robert was intoxicating. I tried to find a way to defuse my interior lustful thoughts. "Did your parents ever question why you never tried out for the Yankees?"

"Actually, I did. I had to know if I was good enough. And I got the callback. I was supposed to report to training camp in Fort Lauderdale the following spring."

"What did your parents think about your decision?"

"They thought I had become a hippie, into drugs, the music crowd, long hair, beard. Blew a lifetime opportunity to play professional sports. 'Are you taking that pot?' my mom would ask, and I'd say, 'Mom you don't take pot, you smoke it. You take drugs, and I don't do either.' I never lied to them. But I could never tell them the entire truth. They accepted that I loved music too. Was there music in your home?"

"No." I wanted to add, *just displeasing voices.* "We had one television set and it sat in our parents' bedroom. I don't even remember having a record player."

"That's hard to imagine. I started my first band at eleven, a New Orleans jazz band, had a trombone and clarinet player, drummer, and I played the trumpet. Hot Lips became my nickname."

I'd take bets at any age he didn't get that nickname from playing an instrument. "Were you any good?"

"No, we were terrible. We only knew one song, 'When the Saints Go Marching In.' At fourteen I did I play the bugle for President Johnson at the International Boy Scout Jamboree in Valley Forge, Pennsylvania, Washington's big battle. Fifty thousand scouts from all over the world came."

"How'd you get that spot?"

"We filled out a form and listed our skills. My answer, I was a musician and had my own band. When it came time for the president to speak, they asked me to play 'To the Colors' as they raised the flag. A picture of me at that jamboree was sent all over the world by the Associated Press."

"You have a way with presidents and getting noticed."

"Yeah, but the picture wasn't me playing the bugle, it was me holding a tape recorder, interviewing my roommates, Dahn and Talhi from Israel. I had snuck in a recorder in my backpack—you weren't allowed to have stuff like that."

There he was breaking another rule … and getting publicity from it.

"I learned a lot about the Mideast from them. Ironic that my work would take me to that part of the world."

I didn't ask questions, but by his expression, I got the sense he might've recently traveled in that direction.

"I found out that everybody in Israel serves in the military."

"Even women?"

"Yeah. If you can't walk, you can be placed for typing; if you can't shoot a gun, you can cook, but everybody serves. Israel is our strongest ally in the entire world."

The album stopped playing and I remembered Robert owed me a story. I don't know why I kept talking; all I wanted to do was get close enough to feel his body next to mine.

"You were going to tell me something about 'Mustang Sally.'"

"That's right, I was. I met Sir Mack Rice, who wrote the song, in high school. I had a rockin' band, called Soul Tones, and it was the first interracial band in America. We had a black sax player and a girl organist. Mack wanted me to go on tour with him, and I considered leaving sports to do it. He told me how the song came about. You want to hear it?"

"Of course, what Sally wouldn't?"

"In his early days, he worked as a staff writer for Stax Records out of Memphis, and he went to visit his friend, Clyde Bowers, who toured as a drummer with Della Reese. You know who she is?"

I shook my head. "Yeah, the jazz and gospel singer. The one that sings like she's been touched by an angel."

"When he arrived, they were finishing a rehearsal, and Clyde told him that Della was buying all the band members a Lincoln Mark IV, a bonus for a profitable year. Clyde said he would rather have the new Mustang. Mack didn't know what a Mustang looked like, so they drove by the Ford dealer to take a peek.

"When Mack saw it," Robert impersonated his voice, "he said, 'Are you shitting me, man? You want that little bitty car when she's gonna get you a big-ass Lincoln? What's wrong with you? That ain't no car for a grown man.'

"The next day at rehearsal, Mack sat in with the band and started making fun of Clyde's Mustang. 'Do dodda dod dodda do, Mustang Mama, you better slow that Mustang down, all you want to do is ride around mama, ride mama ride.' Everyone laughed, but the consensus was that the Mustang riff was pretty cool. He eventually headed back to Memphis and started singing "Mustang Mama" with singer and songwriter Aretha Franklin.

"She played the piano, and he turned it into a full song. Three verses, two choruses, and a piano solo. They decided to pitch the song to the president of the label. As they were about to pitch, when they walked through the door, Aretha whispered in a demanding tone, 'Mack, don't say, Mama! Give her a name! Give her a name!'

"Aretha started playing, Mack sang, 'Do dodda dod dodda do… Mustang Sally, you better slow down, all you want to do is ride around Sally, ride Sally ride.'"

"Cool story."

"Yeah, all because Aretha said to give her a name."

"Do you write music?" I asked.

"I do."

"Do you play any instruments besides the bugle and trumpet?"

"Play about twenty."

"Twenty, really? What do you like to play the most?"

"Baseball."

"Be serious, Hot Lips, what instrument?"

Somewhere in between the music we had lain down on the sofa. As he ran his hands through my hair and over my back, he said, "I like a piano for soft romantic songs, guitar for blues and rock and roll, and drums for smooth jazz. I change the instruments to fit the mood of the music. Rosie, I'm in another mood. Isn't there a more comfortable place we can go?"

This was leading somewhere, and I was unsure who was the aggressor and who was prey. The Hawk looked and acted as suave as my crush Sean Connery in *Diamonds are Forever* as he led me into my own bedroom. I already had candles lit, the bed covers pulled down. The incense had burnt down.

He held me in his tight muscular arms, and I could feel every inch of his body pressed against me. I wanted him to pull me right into his body. He felt like steel covered with soft silk. He picked me up like I was a doll and positioned me anywhere he wanted. Every muscle in my body stretched and yearned for more pleasure than I thought possible. I never believed that could feel so blissful. I lost track of my orgasms. "Ride Sally Ride" took on a new meaning.

We fell asleep in one another's arms. I woke to the smell of bacon frying in the kitchen and the sound of gentle, steady rain, one of my favorite sounds of nature. Before I was out of bed, there was a knock on the door. "I'll get it," Robert called.

Seconds later, he came to me with an envelope in his hand.

"Rosie, a courier, for me. Breakfast in bed will have to be another time. I have to go now, on assignment."

He leaned over, held my hands, and kissed my cheek. Like the day before, he came back for another one on the lips. Before I had time to blink, he was out the door. The rain had evolved to a morning storm. I lay in bed, put my hand over my heart, and prayed, "Dear God, please watch over Robert … Winston … my love." When I went into the kitchen, there was a rose and a poem on the counter.

> *A simple line to tell you,*
> *exactly what I mean,*
> *Yours are the bluest eyes,*
> *This world has ever seen.*

How Robert had time to write a poem, or manifest a rose, was a mystery, but I had proof that he was real, and this wasn't make-believe.

With a Little Help from my Friends

My day had started with an enchanted sensation. It turned into a horrific nightmare. I had to know what was real. Dead man talking to me, the sight of Robert lying on the ground, bleeding from the head.

Gloria, David, and I headed to Neptune to await intel. The three of us sat next to each other around David's desk. I was staring at the phone as if that might make it ring quicker. Gloria was as nervous as I was. She really cared for Robert, not in the same way I did, but nonetheless she was emotionally connected to both of us. David tried to be the voice of reason, offering something to drink and giving me assurance that while things did look bad, we had to stay strong and be ready for any news.

Shortly after we arrived, a call came in from General Lang. After a few minutes David got off the phone and told us about the situation.

"Robert is alive." I let out an emotional sigh and fought to keep back the tears. Gloria hugged me. David tried to speak without emotion, but there was a tear in his eye as well. He cleared his throat. "Unfortunately, Tuck is dead."

Commander Anderson's team had been ambushed as they entered a bordello where opposing forces were said to be located. All nine soldiers in the team had been hit, struck mostly with American-made M16 rifles and three-inch bullets. Six had died. Three had survived. Bowman, hit in the spine, was in critical condition. Jackson had been hit in the shoulder, and Robert in the hand by a Russian-made .45 caliber handgun. Robert and Jackson, both heavily bleeding, had dragged the seven bodies out of the building into a nearby woods. It was in their training: "Never leave a warrior on the battlefield."

By the time Robert had located the buried communicator and sent the longitude and latitude coordinates, the rescue was already underway. Evacuation helicopters had already been dispatched due to my information and landed within minutes with help on the ground. The soldiers were transported to a Navy ship waiting in the waters of Panama.

We were still discussing the turn of events when a communique in the form of fax came in, addressed to the Paranormal Research Department and Covert Operations. It was from a man we only knew as Billy Joe, the current liaison between the president and the NSA. Billy Joe delivered orders from the president and was also his confidant and advisor. He was the same man who had handed Robert's interrogators a note for his release in the Nixon and Lincoln Memorial incident.

David read the fax to us: *I'm sorry for your loss. They were all good men. I think your entire division needs to know what went down and why they were there.*

Due to the destructive power of atomic bombs, the US and Russia have never engaged in one-to-one warfare. Instead, each uses their political philosophies to influence emerging third world nations around the globe. In this case, both countries tried to manipulate the governing of Columbia by backing opposing political factions. Unfortunately, this is the reality of the Cold War.

Commander Anderson's team was sent to capture guerrillas loyal to the late dictator Gustavo Rojas Pinilla, the former leader of Columbia backed by the Soviets. Word was out that a corrupt general, Juan Felipe, was about to overthrow the government. He'd recently made deals with Pablo Escobar, a young drug runner who supplied Felipe with funds in return for future protection. Since we support the current president, Alfonso López Michelsen, the aim was to disrupt the guerilla army. This unauthorized civilian army is exceptionally organized, they act and give the impression of a conventional one.

This ill-fated operation collapsed for the same reason the Bay of Pigs failed fourteen years earlier when John Kennedy tried to assassinate Castro. The CIA relied on foreign informants for undercover sensitive intelligence.

A communique from the Sec Nav will be arriving shortly. You will not recognize the names on it; each US soldier in Bogota had a bogus ID.

Know that your team died honorably in service to their country. I can only imagine the bereavement you must now be experiencing. I share this with you, I knew all of these men. I helped recruit most of them.

Take some form of solace from this, if not for the extraordinary paranormal ability of Casallie and your department's quick action, all would have been lost.

Billy Joe

David put the fax down and addressed us. "The sequence of events that culminated with the rescue illustrates the magnitude and significance of the agency's reliance on paranormal resources in concert with traditional soldiering. The system worked, although the mission failed. Three wounded and six deceased warriors are coming home.

"Rose, you did much more than save three soldiers tonight."

Knockin' On Heaven's Door

DUE TO THE HEAVY BLEEDING, ROBERT RECEIVED OXYGEN UPON arrival on the USS Hancock, a Navy helicopter carrier. The ship was very old, rebuilt three times and near the end of its service. The sickbay was primitive, yet adequate. Robert's training had taught him to meditate, breathe slowly, and focus on staying alive. And he did. The bullet had put a hole in the heel of his hand about the size of a silver dollar; his wrist was practically blown away.

The doctor, Lieutenant Benjamin Stein, told him he could have bled to death in less than a minute if it hadn't been for his army flak jacket. The hollow point bullet had snagged and shredded a piece of cotton from the sleeve, and the material had wrapped around the shell as it entered his hand and wrist. It had jammed in like a cork. After the initial surgery, designed to stop the bleeding, Dr. Stein handed him a bloody, twelve-inch strip of threads and said, "This saved your life."

Even in a sedated state, Robert knew there was more to the story.

ROBERT WAS AIRLIFTED FROM the Navy ship straight to Walter Reed for a second wrist operation. By the third day, he was less sedated and ready for visitors.

Rose entered the room carrying a small bouquet of flowers.

"Hello beautiful. I've been wanting to see you since I arrived. They told me you'd be coming this morning. Sit here, babe." Robert pointed to the side of his bed. "Come and give me a kiss."

Rose placed the flowers on the metal tray beside his bed, leaned over, and kissed him. She sat on the edge of the mattress and tried to avoid his sling and bandaged hand. "Everyone at Meade is so devastated over the losses, but so grateful you came home alive. You gave me a huge scare when I saw you …"

"What do you mean, when you saw me?"

"You were in my vision."

"They told me about the Tuck dialogue, but no one mentioned anything else."

"Yes, I saw you lying with blood all over your face and head. I thought you were dead."

"There's a reason I'm not."

"Do you feel like talking about it?" Rose placed a hand on Robert's chest.

"I've been waiting to talk to you, not much of a military thing, but you'll understand."

"Please, tell me. What is it?"

"Before we entered the whore house, Tuck put us in a flying V formation. He placed me in the back. Connors, in front of me, took at least twenty rounds. The sheer force of the bullets kept him on his feet for several seconds. As I returned fire, someone, something, ripped my left hand from my rifle and slung my arm across my face and positioned my hand and wrist outwardly to shield my temple. At that exact moment I covered my head, I caught the bullet."

"Are you saying you would've been shot in the head?"

"Yes, I would've died instantly without the precise timing and positioning of my hand. It was … unexplainable."

"I have goosebumps … you're describing … a guardian angel …"

"Maybe, I'm not sure. I know I didn't consciously let go of the gun and move my hand to guard my head. I didn't even know there was a gunman on that side of the building. The power of the blast slapped my hand so hard into my head, I went down from the intensity of it."

"That explains your nasty bruise."

"As soon as I took the hit, I turned my hand to let the blood wash over me, to appear I was dead."

"You're describing my image … it was bloody and terrible."

"Yeah, it was so the guerrillas wouldn't come over and make the kill shot before they took off. I was bleeding, but I needed to be still until I was certain it was safe. If I moved, another bullet."

"What are the doctors saying about your hand? Have they told you anything?"

"The Navy ship doc said my military career was over. In a few years, my hand will be cosmetically good. Said I should be able to use my hand for most things unless I played a piano or guitar."

"Oh my."

"Doc went on to say the replacement hinge in my wrist will be unnoticeable. People may notice things like stiffness, spasms, and inability to move three of my fingers independently. Atrophy in my forearm, nothing that long sleeve shirts can't hide. Lang has all but written me off. Even prepared separation papers and arrangements for disability pay."

"How are you taking that?

"I told him I'd be back. I asked him to grant me a six-month leave."

"Did he?"

"Yes, got the leave with pay and status quo. He probably believed it was a hopeless scenario, but he gave me a goal to inspire me. I'll be back."

"Your doctors didn't give you much hope."

"No, but I'll show them they're wrong. I've already created a series of exercises in my mind that'll speed the healing." Robert seemed to have a new-found faith in the power of the Divine, as if someone had singled him out and saved his life. "I'll come back, faster and stronger than ever."

"I believe in you. After all, you're a warrior."

"Rosie, I sure wish I could wrap my arms around you. Turn back time. Pick up where we left off. Caress and explore every part of your body, find out more about the Crazy Stones and all your voodoo magic."

"Wish you wouldn't say voodoo …"

"Yes, ma'am. Babe, I'll never make jokes about what you do again. Because you acted quickly when Tuck came to you, I'm here."

Robert yawned, and his eyelids began to droop. "I think I'm starting to fade. The meds are kicking in. I need to rest."

Tears in Heaven

David enrolled me in the Veritas program at the University of Arizona under the name of Sally Stone. It was the only academic institution in the country in which mediums were scientifically tested and investigated for their legitimacy. If I successfully passed the screening and testing process, I'd become a member of an elite team of Veritas Research Mediums, giving our department more prestige and distinction. David was confident I would be invited; he was just taking precautions in case the Spooks ever came under inspection. Plus, the recognition would also help with my cover as a psychic.

As much as I wanted to attend, I would have preferred to be helping Robert at his home in Winter Park during his recuperation. When I discussed the idea with Robert, he insisted it was my time to fly, become the best in my field, and he would handle his resurgence. I still didn't know exactly where I stood with him ... was I a one-nighter, a one-monther ... I'd like to think I could be ... a foreverer. But there were no guarantees that this warrior would return to me, or to the NSA for that matter.

IN THE PROGRAM, I underwent several stages of questionnaires, interviews, and tests; participated in training in grief psychology, afterlife science, and human subjects' research; and had to demonstrate exceptional ability to report accurate and specific information during double-blind test readings.

I had plenty of time to reflect on angels and warriors, life and death, the spirit world. I questioned who or what determines a Divine intervention? Who decides who lives, who dies, who wins, who loses? Was it God, ancestral karma, or just luck of the draw?

On the outside, it appeared that I could handle my extrasensory gifts. In reality, I struggled with the complexity of functioning in both the physical and spiritual realms. I questioned if my mentors were better skilled at managing their ESP or simply appeared to be because of their age and experience.

In my childhood, there had been no one to talk to about my second sight, my mystical happenings, or my ability to heal and communicate with animals. I tried to talk with my mother at times but that never got me anywhere. She would say I possessed an over-the-top imagination, and if I wasn't careful, I might end up like Joan of Arc. Burned at the stake.

My first mystical incident occurred when I was sixteen. I had enrolled in a spiritual development course at Unity Church. The teacher, Elsie Bodi, was a well-known psychic and author. Paramount Pictures had used her as a consultant on films that featured paranormal phenomena. Because I was a teenager, I needed parental permission to attend the course. My mom gave permission, to my surprise, but made it clear I was never to discuss it.

On the first night of class, Elsie had us using a billet, a concealed question written on a piece of paper. We each wrote a question, folded the paper, and exchanged it with a partner. Each took turns trying to answer the question by relying only on our spiritual senses.

As I held the billet near my forehead, my right eye began to twitch persistently. My partner offered that her eye had quivered earlier in the day, and perhaps I picked up on that and not on her question. I nodded and said, "Maybe." But I thought differently.

We gathered to discuss our billet success, but before taking my seat, I approached Elsie and asked her if she knew why my eye might be fluttering. I was light-headed too. She said she once had known another psychic whose eye twitched when she received communication. I remember thinking, "Oh great, now I'm going to be a twitching-eye psychic." I took a seat.

As she lectured, I continued to have strange sensations until I could no longer remain silent. As I raised my hand to get her attention, my limbs became light. I wanted to speak, but I had lost my voice. My arms began to move and rise in the air as if they contained helium. I felt as if currents of energy were running through my body and that I might turn into a flying nun, like the actress Sally Field.

Elsie told the students, "A spirit has entered Sally." She proceeded to apply what closely resembled the Heimlich maneuver, not once, but three times, until she said I was free or "clear." She said that nothing like that had ever happened in her fourteen years of teaching. On some level, she believed, that my soul had agreed to invite this spirit/angel/entity in. At the time, I thought she was grasping for an explanation. I hadn't invited any such thing in. At least not knowingly.

The incident was mysterious, incomprehensible, confusing, and surreal all at the same time. Although it never was fearful for me, it was unnerving to the thirty onlookers. They didn't sign up for a freak show. Half of the class never returned.

I had read that we only use eleven percent of our brain capacity. I had made a request to God to use more of my brain. If this was the answer, I didn't understand it.

My abilities kept evolving in Elsie's class, probably because it was a safe environment. The class witnessed my first spontaneous mediumship reading. My eye started twitching and my breathing became heavier. Elsie said she heard a voice say, "We're getting ready. We're going to have to go with the flow here. The only feeling I get now is that Sally needs much space around her." Students started moving chairs and within seconds I sat solo facing everyone.

I gave a message for a woman named Melanie, a self-help author who had lost her teenage son in a skiing accident three months earlier. I had no knowledge of this information before delivering the message. The boy wanted his mom to know he was fine, at peace, missed her, and was giving her a big kiss at that moment. He wanted her to feel his love, and to know that Bear, their brown chocolate Lab, was with him.

When I finished, I moved my chair back. Melanie thanked me for the beautiful message and said she had prayed all day to have contact with her son. I was grateful her prayer had been answered but confused as to why I was the vessel.

Perhaps because of those early poignant episodes, I was placed in the distinguished company of famous musicians who also had their own angel connections, which then led me to the NSA, to Robert, to Tuck. But as I thought about it, communication with Tuck had a different kind of mediumship than I had ever experienced. It was unsettling, personal, violent, and a real-time call for help.

I had a feeling there was considerably more to learn and understand about angels, the paranormal, war, and secrets.

Reunited

TWO MONTHS HAD PASSED SINCE I HAD SEEN ROBERT. AS THE wheels touched down at Orlando International Airport, my heart and mind began to race. I couldn't imagine that he yearned for me as I had for him. His life had changed dramatically, going from a twenty-six-year-old super-agent to someone whose future was unknown. His mentor had died. His great uncles had crossed over. He couldn't tell his parents or friends what had happened to him. Instead, he had to lie and say he had been hit by a car while jogging. His letters portrayed him as fine and professing his love and lust for me. I questioned this and would soon find out the truth. I needed to observe in person how his hand was healing and how he was doing.

As I walked out the gate, I tried to remain calm and dignified, but as soon as I saw him, I ran into his arms like a teenager. He greeted me with a warm embrace and kiss. He wanted to hear all about my studies but not until dinner at his favorite restaurant, Korean Tempura Palace. When we arrived, Mrs. Parks, one of the owners, came over and gave Robert a hug. She also hugged me and said, "So Winston, this must be the Sally you've been talking about for weeks." I was elated that she knew my name and that Robert had thought enough of me to share it with his close friends and acquaintances. He was more into me than I thought.

During dinner we made small talk, filling each other in on what we had been doing since our last correspondence. He said nothing about his hand or physical status, and I tried not to stare at his wrist.

We ate rather fast then drove to his home. The house was secluded on forty acres about three miles outside of Winter Park. As we turned into the long, curved driveway, it was a spectacular wooded scene with an abundance of cedar, pines, firs, and palmetto trees. The charm of the brick house, and the gorgeous golden retrievers that came running out, softened the look of the automatic security gate and six-foot barbed wire fence that surrounded the area.

After playing with the dogs, Fred and Ethyl, for a few minutes, we came inside. I was instantly taken by the natural look and feel—cedar ceilings, oak beams, skylight in the living room. I noticed how clean it was and assumed he had a maid. I wondered if she was Swedish, blonde, 5'10" and built like a supermodel or something like that.

To my surprise, Robert carefully lifted and carried me to the bedroom. He was favoring his left hand but compensated admirably. He laid me on the waterbed and stretched out beside me. Both of his strong hands caressed my entire body. If his injury had slowed him up, I certainly didn't notice it. We said a few words during the night, kissing and licking each other and making love until we fell asleep.

The next day started with smells and sounds from the kitchen. I remembered our first night together, and how Robert had been called away in the early morning hours. Now my long-overdue breakfast was being served in bed, accompanied by baby's breath and pink roses.

After eating, we were preparing to go for a long walk and visit the birds when the phone rang. Robert was already out the door. The answering machine came on, and my radar ears deciphered some of the message: "Winston, Bambee here, when am I going to see you,

I'm hoping soon, ready for another massage, you liked it last time …"
I heard enough to deflate my morning and plant suspicion. Bambee
of all names, not Shirley or Irene.

I proceeded out the door and joined Robert in the screened
reserve. He slowly lifted his arms and about twenty finches flocked
to him, from one tip of his outstretched hands to the other. Their
vibrant colors nearly exhausted the senses. The blue canaries were my
favorite. After a few minutes, we sat down on the stone bench.
Watching Robert commune with nature quieted my restless
thoughts. He seemed to communicate with animals on a different
plain than most.

As I watched him with the birds, I recalled a story he had told me.
He was on a mission in Columbia to blow up a cocaine lab, eradicate
the coke labs at the source. Early in his career, he was the point, and
a team of six were trekking through the jungle on what they thought
was good intel about the location of a large coke plant. They came
upon a small rise that blocked the view ahead. Robert gave the
command to halt. He felt an ambush was at hand. He spotted a hawk
sitting high upon a branch.

Within an instant of thinking that he wanted to see what the
hawk saw, he felt that he had become the bird, high in the air,
weightless and without movement. He spotted danger, a trap, just
over the rise. As a result, his team split up and circled around the
trap. The mission was successful. They blew up the plant without
alerting the drug cartel. No ambush or lost lives.

When he recounted that story, he had seemed transported back
to that bird moment when he came to that scene. I thought to myself,
Bird Medicine. At Neptune, Robert was revered as an operative for
his sixth and seventh sense. Just one more intriguing thing about him
to cope with.

ROBERT PONTIFICATED ON TUCK as I observed all the winged creatures. Tuck had encouraged him to embrace poetry, music, and the love of animals, said it would balance the violent energy needed to be a warrior. He had been a special warrior, had understood the yin and yang, that there was no fast without slow. He had been the oldest of the division and loved and admired by all.

Robert told me about a time he had returned from an assignment in which he had had to take a life or die himself in order to complete the mission. When he came home, he became obsessed with saving a baby mockingbird that had fallen from its nest. He had even given the bird a name since he was incessantly tending to him: John Lennon.

He couldn't leave John in the aviary, but since birds learn to fly from their parents, he carefully brought him into the reserve every day to observe the others. For more than a week, Robert fed him with an eyedropper and kept him warm. He knew that when the bird was able to fly, he would be strong enough to feed himself. Robert felt humbled by the whole experience.

It was interesting how he dealt with the dichotomy in his life. He had taken a human life and decided to save and nurture another life. I suspected Tuck was behind his inspiration.

Robert told me that he was on schedule. I did not interrupt, but I thought, *On schedule for what?* He said that he planned to be back to work in several months. He didn't care what the doctors had projected: the power of his mind was greater.

"I've been working diligently on my own therapy. I disposed of my meds early on and started exercising my hand all day." He shared the details, and I wasn't surprised when he brought up his childhood hero.

"Every morning I take a baseball and force it into my crimped-up hand to stretch the tendons. I pictured the time I witnessed Mickey

Mantle up at the plate as a pinch hitter. He'd been injured for weeks and the team needed one run to win. When he swung, he fell to one knee from the pain and still managed to muscle the ball over the wall for a home run. For it to count, he had to rise and run around the bases. Every step of the way you could tell he was in agony. The entire team waited for him at home plate. That memory pushed me: if he could overcome his pain and accomplish that feat, I could ignore mine and attain my goal."

Robert was earnest and made no mention of massages, and certainly no massages with happy endings, as I had been imagining. "I have something important to talk to you about," he said. "We only have one more day together before you fly back, and I want to address our relationship."

This was not going to be good. I had that familiar sinking feeling that I associated with my mother. When everything was going well, something was bound to drop and shatter it. I expected Robert, the notorious Hawk, to say he was not ready to date one person. He had the Bambees, or he was going to bring up the agency's rules on dating.

He reached out with both hands. I touched them lightly, aware of the steel hinge in his left wrist. His eyes softened.

"Babe, it's time! I want to move forward with us. I want us to only see each other. How do you feel about that?"

His words caught me off guard. Was he speaking from the heart? Had the bad boy been transformed? What about his girls? Or had his injury slowed him down from the different-girl-every-night scene?

"Rose, on this planet we use words."

Don't Stop Believin

ROBERT'S MEDICAL LEAVE GAVE HIM TIME TO CONSIDER HIS alternatives, to see if he still had the desire to do the job. He had to be 100 percent if he was to continue with the agency; 99 percent meant second place, and second place in his line of work meant death. His immediate goal was to show General Lang he was ready for active duty. He did not have a definitive plan, but Robert was determined to show everyone that mattered he was prepared for anything.

On Monday, June 7, 1976, nearly six months after being shot, Robert walked into the office of ADCO, and announced, "I'm back."

With a fixed gaze, General Lang said, "I thought you were permanently disabled."

With his left hand, Robert grabbed him by the shirt and tie, picked him up, and said, "Excuse me, sir, does it look like I'm disabled? I can do anything with my left hand that I could ever do. I'm better at it because I'm no longer right-handed; I'm ambidextrous."

The general, astonished and somewhat disheveled from Robert's hoisting, said, "Okay, okay, I get your point, now put me down if you want me to activate your file. I read the dossier on you. How the fuck did you get so much strength in your injured hand?" His eyes softened, and he had a barely noticeable smile. Robert knew he was back. If General Lang wanted something, he knew how to make it happen. "You'll need to have Lieutenant Commander Spears sign the discharge release from medical leave."

"I really don't care what the doc says."

"Well, unfortunately, there's a small mountain of paper that needs the lieutenant commander's signature. You've convinced me, I'm sure you can persuade him."

Robert took that to mean, do whatever it takes to get the job done. He went to see Lieutenant Commander Spears. At first, the doctor was hesitant, and Robert did the same thing he had done with General Lang: he grabbed him with his bad hand and lifted him a foot-and-a-half off the ground, then said, "Sign the damn release."

"I can't in good faith put you back on assignment knowing that you may not be ready."

"Doc, don't take this the wrong way. I can kill you right now with only my left hand. Of course, I'm not going to, but you need to understand that I'm not disabled. I can do anything with this hand." Robert put the doctor down. "Don't take this personally, but you were wrong, and so were twenty other doctors."

Spears shook his head and said, "I never thought in a million years that you'd be able to use that hand, the nerve damage was so extensive." He pulled out Robert's medical file and displayed the x-rays on a lightbox attached to the wall behind him. "This is a miracle. The nerves were severely damaged. They just don't grow back by themselves. If you pass the pin test, I will sign the release."

Robert knew the drill. He placed his hand behind his back. The doctor randomly pricked each finger then tested for hot and cold sensory acuity. There was no sign of sensory damage. Spears signed the paperwork. "When we have time, I'd like to hear how you made a complete recovery."

With the first two hurdles cleared, Robert had to get a psychiatric evaluation for the third and final step to active duty. Having the blessing of the ADCO and the reluctant, yet official, release from the lieutenant commander, Robert now had to face his attractive frenemy, Dr. Michelle Thompkins, perhaps the only female on base who had never fallen for his charms.

AS ROBERT ENTERED Dr. Thompkins office, he noticed a picture of an army captain on her desk. She also was wearing an engagement ring.

"Hello, Robert, so nice to see you again." She said with a long face and sad eyes. "We've all missed you here. Six months is a long time without you."

Robert noticed that everyone seemed to be cautious with their words around him. He understood that his return brought back to all of Neptune the shock and horror of losing seven warriors. Bowman had died days after his return. Robert thought this had to stop. What happened, happened. It was time to move on.

"You know the routine," Dr. Thompkins said. "Dr. Head notified me of your medical release. Excellent news. Now all that stands in your way for active duty is my evaluation."

"It's good to be back, Michelle, and yes I know the procedure. I'm sorry I was so difficult last time. I'll try to be more congenial, although it's not my strong suit."

"Never mind that, you and I have a respectable relationship. I know what it means to be in your shoes."

"Excuse me, but how could you possibly know what it's like?"

"I don't have to jump off the Empire State Building to know it would hurt. I'm painfully aware of the shock and horror of your last mission. We're all grieving the loss of Tucker and his team. I want to go back to that night. The night you got shot, how did it feel?"

Before Robert spoke, he fell silent for a moment. He had relived this moment every day for six months. He did not want to talk about it. So instead he spoke only of his encounter with a bullet.

"Well, imagine you get a splinter in your finger. It hurts, right? All you think about is that damn splinter. You can be at a movie, at dinner, and all you're thinking about is that splinter. Now imagine that splinter is the size of a marble and entered your body at four hundred degrees going twenty-two hundred miles an hour. That's what it felt like getting shot. It sucked."

"I'm more interested in your thoughts and feelings about the entire experience. Do you feel different today than six months ago?"

Once again, he atypically fell quiet for a moment as he leaned over and swung one of the steel balls in Newton's cradle that was on her desk. He was determined to talk only about his involvement, not what happened to the others.

"Before, I felt like I was invincible, that I could survive anything. I was trained to think that way …"

Dr. Thompkins realized he was not going to talk about the ambush in Bogota and changed the line of interaction.

"Still not what I'm trying to get at." She sighed. "So let me lead you. You're a million-dollar asset to the agency, considered the top in your military occupational specialty. Suddenly everything changes. The NSA writes you off. All your dreams gone … you can no longer be a musician, play baseball, or perform your duties. Did you wonder what you were going to do with your life?"

"No, I knew I was coming back. I knew the doctors were wrong!"

"Wasn't that denial?"

"Well, it happened. I'm back. It's not denial if it's true. If you need a word for it, it's confidence. Maybe all of you are in denial about what really happened. The docs were wrong, I was right. I also think something else came into play. Divine Providence … a guardian angel."

"Interesting. Did you come up with that yourself?"

"When I got shot, I had an angel protecting me. That's why I'm still here. I won't go into details, but I know I wasn't spared to sit on the sidelines and watch the world go by. I believe I have more earthly missions to do. There's a great deal of evil in the world and only a handful of warriors willing to wage war against it."

"I've never heard you talk like this before. Have you told anyone else this, your guardian …?"

"One other person."

"I'm going to go out on a limb and say it was the angel girl."

"You know her?"

"Yes, I've seen her on occasion. All I can say. I also know that you and Rose have developed a special relationship, the word is out on you two. And as usual, it seems you get away with things that others can't."

"And how does that make you feel, doctor?" Robert said with a sideways smile.

"Touché," she replied, also with a smile.

"I don't think I want to talk about my relationship right now."

"Robert, you know that everything you tell me is private. I'm bound by my ethics to repeat nothing. All I'm assigned to do is tell Dr. Head if you're fit for duty or not."

"Well, Rose and I have become close. We wrote to each other, saw each other as frequently as possible. She has recently moved to Winter Park and has set up shop there. I may be falling in love with the angel girl. I'm going to ask her to move in with me, and don't ask how that makes me feel."

"Okay, I won't, but if you ever wish to talk about those feelings, you know where I am. We don't always have to talk about violence. I can see the yin and yang force between you two. Let's go back to our topic. One last thing, are you afraid of getting shot again?"

"Of course, who wouldn't be? I was afraid of getting shot the first time."

"I'm glad to hear that. It shows me you're in the game and not delusional."

"Nobody wants to get shot. The psychological effect of watching my team die before me was motivating. I'll be more aggressive in the future. I don't want to die, and I don't want to be shot again. If there's going to be a battle, I now know, don't be second. Shoot first."

"I think I have enough information. Dr. Head will have my assessment this afternoon."

As Robert walked out, he turned back and said, "Congratulations on the engagement. He's a lucky man."

Black Magic Woman

ON MY DAYS AWAY FROM NSA, I WAS SALLY STONE, A CERTIFIED research medium. I moved in with Robert in the spring of '77. Early on, it was known throughout the agency that we dated and broke the rules; now we had progressed to living with each other and it was accepted. After Robert's return to work, he had more support and encouragement than ever before, even with affairs of the heart. Except for the secretary pool, who were all disheartened that he was no longer available.

My office for my cover, Sally's Spiritual Connection, was conveniently located on Winter Park's busiest street, Park Place. It was within walking distance from the Langford Resort Hotel. As Winston Forester, Robert played piano regularly at the Langford when he was off duty. Gloria often arranged to spend a day or so down south so she could sit in with Robert and resurrect her old desire to be a singer. My world felt quite complete being with my love, having my best friend near, and with my new business.

Robert helped decorate my business space. We found handmade bent willow chairs made, fittingly enough, by a Kentucky artist. They were perfect chairs for giving or receiving a reading: comfortable, grounding, and natural. A nearby antiques and linen store had about everything else I needed to create a warm and welcoming environment.

Word had spread of my abilities and gifts, and there was no shortage of upscale clients when the snowbirds came down. Sometimes I thought my clients expected someone with more of a gypsy look than I had. Even with my third eyes, Egyptian motifs, incense, sage, and patchouli perfume, I still came across looking reserved and normal.

I worked by appointment only and had an extensive waiting list. One particular Tuesday, a distraught woman named Carolyn came in, and I sensed I should make an exception and take the walk-in.

"Excuse me, I don't have an appointment, but I'm in dire need of help. Are you able to give me a reading? It's about—"

I stopped her in time. "Please don't say anything else. I work best when I don't have any information up front.

"Carolyn, do you want a Mediumship or a Psychic Reading?"

"I'm not sure. Can you explain the difference?"

"Mediumship is when you want to talk specifically to a departed loved one. A spiritual psychic reading addresses life issues such as romance, career, or life direction."

In a cracking voice, she said, "I have no idea what I need."

"Okay, so let's go with the psychic." Since I was through for the day and had time, I agreed to work with her. I typically asked the client to think about questions ahead of time and write them down. I didn't look at the questions, but the exercise made for a stronger session. Most times I answered the questions without the client having to ask them. In this case, Carolyn didn't have time to prepare, so I went with what I received clairvoyantly and clairaudiently.

I began with my usual blessing: "Dear Mother-Father God, Creator Source, we ask for the highest guidance for Carolyn, who comes to me now. I ask to connect to Carolyn's highest guides of light, love, and truth, her angels, the archangels, ascended masters, and enlightened loved ones. I ask to get my own stuff out of the way. I ask that the reading be specific, relevant, helpful, healing, and for the highest good for all. And so it is."

Immediately, I saw a beautiful blonde-haired, blue-eyed girl, youthful and happy; then my vision switched to a much darker scene, a dungeon-looking room with no way to escape. I got the name Angel, Anna, or Angela. I asked, "Does this make any sense, are you trying to find a child?"

"Yes, yes, her name is Angela. She's my twelve-year-old niece, missing for twenty-four hours. Please tell me she's alive."

"She's alive. But they're telling me she's been kidnapped." I hesitated, then decided to share what I had heard by thought even though I felt uncomfortable. "Something having to do with her virgin blood on the solstice." I knew the celestial event was only days away. I went on with the reading. "I see a dark red symbol, an upside-down cross, and a pentagram star. Do you know what that means, Carolyn?"

"No, I'm afraid I don't."

"It stands for devil worshipping, I believe."

"Oh God! Oh God! What should I do?"

"Let me go on and see what else comes through ... an attractive female is leading a small gathering. It's dark, late at night. I'm getting a name, Napol ... eon. Does Napoleon mean anything to you?"

"No, I mean, of course, I know of the French leader Napoleon ..."

"Okay, not Napoleon but something shorter like, Napol. Make note of that name, it's coming in strong and there must be some link or connection."

The sitting ended with both of us concerned about Angela. I tried to comfort Carolyn without giving false hope or coloring the situation. I didn't see death. My spirit guides rarely gave me that kind of information, but I did sense danger and urgency. Carolyn said her sister, Angela's mom, had already notified the police about her disappearance. She asked if I would be willing to talk to them if they wanted. I said yes and told her I had helped the FBI before in unsolved crimes and missing persons cases.

Directly after she left, I called Robert at headquarters. He knew what to do and assured me we could find this child before the solstice. There were only three days until a young girl might be sacrificed.

By the time I arrived home, Robert had convinced the ADCO to arrange FBI support and a jet to transport him back to Florida. He had persuaded General Lang the case was worth taking even though it was not in their usual playbook.

THE FBI FOUND a close match to Napol, just missing the "i." An occult leader named Roxanne Napoli lived in Winter Park, in the same neighborhood as the missing girl. Informants in the field had followed the rise in devil-worshiping cults, especially in and around Orlando. Napoli, a thirty-year-old female, had a coven in the area and was suspected of Quaalude distribution as well as drinking blood from animals and other satanic rituals.

Robert explained the connection between Quaaludes and devil worship. "Often the leaders of the sect, commonly female, distribute them and ultimately control their coven with hypnotic drugs and sex."

"Sex ..." I said.

"Yeah, young men become the seducers' servants as well as their bodyguards. Here's a picture of Roxanne Napoli." From a folder he pulled a photo of a hot, seductive-looking woman, a mix between a Vogue model and a Playboy bunny. She had long auburn hair, big brown eyes that that were deep and sultry, and a long, lean body with large breasts. It was hard to imagine she would be associated with kidnapping a virgin for her blood. I laid down the picture and asked, "What's your plan?"

The FBI had located a family real estate development business.

They had an upscale address, no storefront strip mall office. Napoli Development, Inc., had a free-standing, two-story brick building. The parking lot was landscaped with lighted palms and lush gardens. The entire place reeked of money. Judging by the cars in the visiting parking spaces, so did their clients.

"I'm going to attempt to infiltrate the cult. We have little time. I know Roxanne works at her dad's business. I'll try to win her confidence quickly, see if a ceremony is planned. Babe, I'm on my way out the door to have a fake tattoo put on my arm. The one you sketched for me."

"The inverted cross and pentagram. What, so she'll think you're into the same fascination as she?"

"Yeah, you can see the tip of it here on her arm." Robert pointed to the photo.

"Yes, I do." I also noticed her plunging neckline and cleavage.

"I'm going to engage in whatever it takes, even if it means …"

"Don't say anymore." I knew what he was alluding to. "I'll see you when you return."

Robert left around noon and arrived back home at 2:00 a.m. I heard him shower before he crawled into bed. He wasn't his usual self. He said, "Let's talk in the morning and I'll tell you what went down. I found Roxanne and I think I've gained her trust." I knew exactly what went down. Even after bathing, he reeked of musty perfume and the smells of after-sex. To make matters worse, it was the first time since we had begun living together that we didn't partake in lovemaking of some kind.

He gave me a soft kiss. "'Night. I love you."

"I love you too." I tried to sound sincere and unbothered.

We both woke up seducing each other, unsure which one of us had initiated it. My orgasms were intensified and more in number than usual. It might have been a release from the built-up tension, dealing with another, but necessary, woman.

Over coffee, Robert seemed anxious to confide his previous day's activities. "Rosie, this is uncomfortable to talk about, but it's all about trying to save a child with little time."

"I know you had sex with her."

"Yes, I found her at the Napoli real estate office. I walked in and pretended to be new to the area and looking for a home. She's a business manager by day. I recognized her and spotted the tip of her tattoo below her shirt sleeve. I approached her desk …"

"With your flirtatious smile and muscular body, how could she not seduce you?"

"Can I tell the story? I started asking questions. I made sure she saw my tattoo when I reached for a pen. That led to … how many details do you want?"

"Go on," I said in a calm, superficial tone. "I'll tell you when I've had enough."

"My plan was to let her seduce me. I sensed that she controls men by her appearance. And her overconfidence and narcissism would lead her to believe she had one more boy toy to play with. We started talking, and she shared she was taking the rest of the day off and wondered if I'd join her for a glass of wine or a bite to eat. We ended up at her apartment."

"And let's see … you said, 'Isn't there some place more comfortable that we can go to?'"

Robert ignored my comment and continued. "Well, she was the seducer, and part of her foreplay was transferring a Quaalude from her mouth to mine to set the mood."

"How'd you pretend you were taking it?"

"In this case, I had to lessen the effects … because I couldn't take it out straightaway without being detected. And this led …"

"Okay, Casanova, I'm visual and psychic, can we save the

remainder for another time?"

"But, Rosie, in that short time together …" *I knew what he could do in one hour, let alone twelve.* "I gained access to her phone numbers, car and license plates, addresses. All now handed over to the FBI."

"Any signs of Angela?" I asked.

"No."

"Any mention of the solstice?"

"Kind of. She mentioned a private ritual on Saturday, and that I might be interested in attending. Baiting me, she said she needed to spend more time with me before formally inviting me."

"So, let me get this straight, you're telling me you may not be home this evening."

"Yeah, I may not come home."

ROBERT ARRIVED HOME at 4:00 a.m. When he entered the bedroom, I wanted to say, "Take a shower, or two. Better yet, sleep on the couch." But I didn't. I kept telling myself that this was all for the greater good.

The next morning he told me he was "in good graces with Roxy." I was not thrilled he'd given this woman a nickname. He'd been invited to the service and given its location and time. The plan was go in alone with no arms, just hidden back-up. Contact mics would be concealed in the shrubs around the foundation, taped to the wall and to the basement window. This would allow the conversation to be heard and transmitted to a nearby surveillance van. If disturbance was detected, back up would to go in, hard. Things were going down at midnight.

TWELVE O'CLOCK PASSED. One o'clock. The solstice was over. The phone finally rang.

"Hey babe, it's me. We're a powerful team."

I thought I knew what that meant, and Robert confirmed it. Angela was safe and home. He was calling me from the ER waiting room.

Robert shared the night's events. People had gathered for the ceremony, about twenty altogether, in the cave-like room where all the windows were sealed and blacked out. The women were dressed in skimpy lingerie; the men wore hooded robes. Robert was given one to wear. Everyone stood in a semi-circle in front of a table, a long wooden door on top of a cinder block where a young, blonde, naked girl lay, draped with only a purple veil. Her hands had been crossed above her head, palms touching, and her mouth taped. Her feet had been tied similarly to her hands but not as tightly. The young girl, Angela, was motionless, either drugged or in shock. Four men guarded Roxanne and the altar, one on each corner, where a handful of violent weapons lay—axe, knife, hammer, and ice pick.

Different people took turns reading until Roxanne took over. She spoke Latin scripture from a pulpit as her flock mumbled words back to her, intermittently mingled with a two-tone chant. Twelve feet away, Robert was keenly aware that a coven's leader was the only one allowed to move on the virgin. He didn't know whether she was going to bleed the girl for ritual blood or kill her. He knew time was critical, though, and he didn't plan to wait to see what Roxanne's intentions were.

He had figured that two of the four guards would go after him when he made his move. The others would most likely protect Roxanne. He studied Roxanne's movements and noticed that when she read the scripture, she took a breath before each new sentence and focused on the words for at least a couple of seconds—the effect of the Quaaludes. In her drugged state, it would take several seconds for her to react to any new stimuli. He had made his move on her next breath, diving onto the table and kicking the guard on the left side in the groin. In the same motion, he grabbed two of the weapons and stretched his body out to shield Angela's. As he rolled over her, he had hit two guards, still in their respective corners, with an axe and a hammer. The fourth guard ran.

In seconds, the place was in a panic. Most of the coven had run out to a waiting group of state troopers. However, Roxanne joined the fight and stabbed him in the lower back with the pick. Robert theorized that this had been more about his betrayal of her than about the girl. The pick wound was shallow; no vital organs were damaged. He threw an elbow to Roxanne's head and she had dropped to the ground.

He had never lost touch with Angela. When backup had burst in, he was still protecting her with his body. Florida state troopers had taken custody of her and gotten her home to her family.

Robert said he was proud of me, and that I had saved another soul, this time a child. It was he who had rescued her and taken the risk; I had just passed on the information to set the whole thing in action. I had only been the messenger, not the power source.

Run for Your Life

Under the full moon, I built a spring fire and waited for Robert to arrive home. The fire took longer than usual to catch. The goldens were right there with me. My thoughts were all over the place.

Back at headquarters, they thought Robert and I were quite a team. We had saved a girl and broken up a cult ring. But this team partner was having problems. I understood intellectually that Robert had slept with the cult leader to gain her trust, and that the plan probably wouldn't have worked without the illusion that he had succumbed to her sexual desires and control. Emotionally, something had shifted in our love-making. It was less passionate, less playful, more forced … just off.

Flashes of Roxanne frequently popped into my mind. I knew how skilled Robert was, how he brought me pleasure, and I pictured him using those same moves on another woman. I was worried that his old playboy ways might resurface. He had reassured me things were different now that we lived together. After being shot, he had different priorities and realized that his actions had consequences for others. Yet he hadn't considered this when he decided to have sex with Roxanne. It had been meaningless to him. But it was not meaningless to me.

The constant danger that surrounded Robert when he went out on assignment was another concern, more than full-moon jitters. I was building my life around a man who could be gone in a second. I thought I might be focusing too much on the sexual aspects to avoid facing my fear of him dying and leaving me.

The goldens left my side and ran toward the gate, signaling that Robert was home. He greeted me with a strong hug and a passionate kiss and a slap on the butt as he walked away to change clothes.

When he returned, he took over as the fire master. After small talk about the weather and the dogs, I expressed some of my fears.

Robert responded. "While it's true that some of my assignments are *Mission Impossible*, some are also like *The Andy Griffith Show* and *Dukes of Hazzard.*"

I had a hard time following his television vernacular comparisons, so he explained. "Well, I think *Mission Impossible* speaks for itself. Andy, a sheriff without a gun, so relatively safe. The *Dukes* was about fast cars and southern boys having fun."

It seemed he'd purposefully forgotten to mention James Bond, the sexy spy who slept with all the hot women. Perhaps he sensed his sleeping with the enemy was still an issue with me. I told him his analogies were too frivolous for the gravity of what he did. After all, he was one of the few remaining from his team; the rest were dead!

"Rosie … I have a *Dukes of Hazzard* story, one with no violence. My version is called *Johnny Ray & the AMX* … and it's coming live from Rose Casallie's birth city, the drug hub of the loose buckle of the bible belt: Lexington, Kentucky."

"Lexington … a drug hub?"

"Yeah, the gateway to Nashville, Indianapolis, Chicago, Detroit, Cincinnati, and Louisville. Cocaine originates in Columbia, ships through Mexico City, from there it's transported to Lexington, the distribution point. The cartel uses a bogus coal business as a cover because it's not unusual for them to have a large amount of money transactions."

Ethyl, the older of the goldens, came over by the fire and put her head on my lap as Robert continued.

"I made friends with a fellow named Allen Bentley. He frequently visited a dance club where my band played, Pete & Lenny's. He was a good-looking guy, athletic, girls dug him, guys wanted to hang out with him because he was cool. Under different circumstances, I would've been friends with him. He was a friendly guy, but he was a dealer. Not an ordinary street dealer; a large-scale wholesale distributor."

"You make it sound like a legitimate business."

"It was an illicit one. Well-organized and profitable. He enlisted my help to move a large quantity of coke. As it turned out, this guy wasn't the kingpin, definitely on the lower rungs of the cartel, and simply transported the drugs to Lexington. It took me several weeks to figure out the who, what, and where of his job. Allen gave us nicknames so we would come across as good ole southern ole boys as opposed to sophisticated city slickers. I was Willy John; he was Johnny Ray.

"Has a *Dukes of Hazard* ring to it."

"My assignment was to follow the coke and see where it went, track the money, and pass the information on. We would deliver the cocaine, receive large shipments of cash, and deposit the money in a Lexington bank under a dummy corp. The bank had branches in other states, where other people would take out the cash.

"On one of our runs, the people we bought from decided to get greedy. They planned to fake the sale, probably kill us, take the money, and keep the drugs. The money belonged to a syndicate, not Johnny Ray, and if we didn't show up with the cocaine, they'd either kill us or our family."

Horrible visions floated in my mind as Robert poked at the fire. Young Fred had nudged his way onto part of my lap. Two full-grown goldens were snuggled up to me by the fire. If not for the topic of conversation, it could have been the setting of a Norman Rockwell portrait. Robert paused while he threw on a few more logs.

"We made the buy; we checked every bag. I knew this big guy standing behind me was about to pull a gun. Don't know how, but I did. When I closed the lid on the metal case containing the drugs, I pushed Johnny Ray, who was standing next to me, out of the way. In one motion I turned, swung the case, and rammed the guy holding the gun on the side of his head as hard as I could. Johnny Ray picked up a table and slammed it into another guy, pinning him against the wall before he had the chance to pull his gun. We grabbed the case, jumped in the car, and the chase begun. Thankfully, that day I had chosen to drive my '72 AMX."

"What's an AMX?"

"American Motors, a two-seater car, about the size of a Corvette. Fastest production car made in America! Mine was hot red with a big racing stripe down the middle. We were traveling ninety-plus, watching our mirrors, when we spotted a car gaining on us. We knew it was them. I hit the gas hard, aiming to reach Valdosta before our pissed-off enemies did."

"Why Valdosta?"

"It was the closest city of any size to us, we needed to get off the highway. We had a forty-mile stretch with no exits. Normally, it's a ninety-minute run from Jacksonville to Valdosta. We did it in under an hour. By the time we arrived, the speedometer had reached one hundred and thirty-five. We blew by every car."

"What about police?"

"No police around. If there had been, we would've been caught, busted, and gone to jail."

"What about your 'get out of jail card'?"

"Would've happened, but the release might've taken several days. Most likely we would have been beaten up first by a bunch of Georgia cops.

"My AMX came with a four hundred-and-two horsepower stock, but our guys bored that out and added another eighty horsepower."

"I don't know what that means."

"It had almost five hundred horsepower, making it one of the fastest cars on the planet. By the time we got to Valdosta, we had lost them. Doing the math in my head, I knew we were safe, thirty miles ahead of them. But before I could slow down, we came upon a stretch of road that had a sharp rise in it. When we hit the wave, the car went airborne."

"What did that feel like?"

"Slow motion … We were about four feet off the ground, but in those couple of seconds, it seemed like ten minutes. I saw the word 'death' written in smoke. I thought, 'it's over, we're done.'"

"What was Johnny Ray doing?"

"He was yelling and praying, 'Oh God, we're going to die … our father who art in heaven …' After flying through the air, we came down front end first. Fortunately, the car crumpled to absorb the shock. The welded seams over the wheel wells split open, and the engine laid practically flat on the ground, still running. I turned it off and we jumped out, thinking the car would blow up any minute."

"Did it?"

"No. I found out later that in real life, most cars in crashes don't explode. Just in the movies. We ran from the car, forty or fifty feet away. I think we were a little disappointed that it didn't blow up. We flagged a car, got a ride into town and were dropped off at the only restaurant around. Every redneck in Georgia must have been there. We stood out—long hair, beards, well-dressed, physically fit, looked like we had money. The waitress threw the menus on the table, left, and we heard her boss say, 'Don't serve them.' I saw these big ole fat guys coming toward us. I said, 'Johnny Ray, we need to go.'

"He said, 'No, I ain't going. No redneck is going to chase me out of any place. I'm getting something to eat. "I said, 'We need to go now! They have bats. There're six of them. They want to kill us.'"

"I take it you all left?"

"We left, but we didn't open the door. At the last second, when they made a move toward us, we ran through the door, knocking it off its hinges. They came after us."

"I know that they couldn't catch you! Did they catch Johnny Ray?"

"No, he was an athlete too. Not as fast as me, but fast. We ran into the woods, I said follow me, and he did."

"What happened to the coke?"

"We had ditched the case in the woods earlier. I knew where to hide it so my team could retrieve it. We went on foot to Jacksonville, took us two days. We were at the airport and about to buy plane tickets when I said, 'Johnny, are you holding?'

"He said, 'I have a little coke on me.'

"I said, 'Come to the bathroom with me. Get rid of it. They're going to search us.' He said, 'How do you know?'"

"Yeah, why would they search you guys?"

"Some stewardesses at the time had let me know about the airlines profiling passengers due to the latest hijackings. The counter girls had a list of things to observe. If they saw any three or four signs on the list, they had a silent button to call security.

"Number one: Long hair. Ding.

"Number two: Beards. Ding.

"Number three: Traveling without luggage. Ding, ding, ding, ding.

"No doubt we'd be hauled into a room, patted, and searched."

"Did it happen?"

"It did, and if we had kept that coke we would've been in another big mess."

"What about the car?"

"I called American Motors and told them my car was still under warranty and had a little problem."

I laughed. "A little problem …? And I thought this was your idea of a non-dangerous assignment."

"I said, 'The car's on I-75 about four miles south of Valdosta, and I think the wheel came off.' They said they'd pick it up and try to take care of it. Two weeks later they called, said my car was ready. I couldn't believe it, looked like it never happened. They rewelded everything, put it all back together. They even rebuilt the engine with the extra horsepower."

"Wouldn't you love to know the mechanic's thoughts when they brought the car in … Yeah, a wheel fell off all right." Just as I asked, "Whatever happened to Johnny Ray?" the alarm went off, bright lights came on, and both dogs ran towards the front of the house, barking loudly and fiercely. Robert told me to sit still and he would check it out. A few moments later the trio returned. A raccoon had tried to climb the chain-link fence.

"Now, where was I?"

"You were telling me what happened to Johnny Ray."

"When everything went down, about a year later, he went down with it. 'Don't do the crime, if you can't do the time.' He got a plea deal; eight years or eighty years. He turned state's evidence and is serving eight."

Robert paused. "I liked him. That's one of the problems of going undercover. You live it. When you live it, you live it."

"Was it a big bust?"

"About a hundred and sixty people got busted altogether, between

Canada and the United States. Twenty-seven in Lexington, the receivers and the money people. We took an estimated thirty million dollars' worth of coke a month off the street."

"That's a lot." I was about to ask him more about the Lexington connection when the new cordless phone rang and I answered it.

"Hello."

"Sally, this is Mom. I could die at any minute. I might not even make it through this phone conversation. You don't have to come home if you don't want to. I understand."

I rolled my eyes with suspicion and motioned to Robert I was heading back to the house. "You said you could die any moment?"

"Yes, Sally. I have a ninety-eight percent blockage in my heart! I'm having surgery in a week. It would be nice to see you before I go under the knife. After all, I'm your mother. I gave birth to you and haven't seen you for years."

Crazy

ROBERT FOLLOWED ME BACK TO THE HOUSE. WHEN I WAS OFF THE phone, he asked, "Are you going home? I heard you say your mother may die."

"No, I have no plans to." I debated if I should tell him that my mother played the death card every couple of years. And that I had never recovered from the college summer when my mother evicted me for accidentally breaking a gallon jar of marbles. She had yelled, cried, and screamed like I had killed her cat. She had also spanked me on my ass as I leaned over to collect the loose marbles while she was clearly losing hers.

Calling her Betty Ann and using the C-word—Crazy—was enough to provoke her to throw me out, start a distortion campaign against me, and deliver a formal eviction notice. The last thing I wanted was Robert to think I might be like her. He would leave me for sure. It was probably best to wait and share the loose marbles story some other time.

"Aren't you concerned?" Robert continued. "I don't want you to have regrets if something did happen to her. You should go. You're off-book until mid-month and that gives you several weeks to spend there."

Jeez, Louise, did he say several weeks ... was he trying to get rid of me? I decided I would take his advice and go home for a few days. I knew much more about my mother's mental illness than my earlier days with her. I had Robert in my life. NSA was my family. My mom could actually die. Even through all the craziness and vindictiveness, I still loved her and only wanted her to love me.

I just hoped that I was not going from one witch scenario to another.

THE FOLLOWING WEEK IN PARIS, KENTUCKY

When I walked through my parents' front door my mother wanted me to pet her cats, Drifter and Fuzzyface, before I could set my bags down. It had been so long since I had been there, I had forgotten what a creative decorator and immaculate housekeeper my mother was. You could eat off her floors. She told me to go say hello to my father. He would be glued to his recliner.

The sound of a blaring television told me his location. I went into the family room and gave him a hug. He offered to make me a Hot Brown and cheesecake while I was home and said that there were chili dogs from Tastee Freez in the fridge. I didn't have the heart to tell him that I no longer ate that kind of food.

"Dad, I plan to stay several days after the surgery and help out around the house, so you can tend to Mom at the hospital. How serious is it? Could she really die at any minute?"

"She's too mean to die," he said with a smirk.

I couldn't tell if my father was joking, had been in the vodka early, or his dementia had worsened where he lost his inhibitions to express his true thoughts. He continued, "You might want to be careful what you say around her. She's on the edge."

Shot nerves, I thought to myself. *When is she not?*

I returned to the kitchen and found my mother nervously cleaning the spotless counters. She paused and said, "Sally, I must tell you something. Your brother Thomas heard Jimmy Swaggart on television, and that set him off. Ever since, he believes he has committed the unpardonable sin, whatever that is. Something about cursing God in his head."

Taking a drag off her cigarette, dish rag in hand, she continued in a rapid speed, "He made a visit to Brother John and went on and on about the 'pain in his head.' After that, your father and I took him to the Central Baptist Hospital. He scared us to death with his nonsense. They put him in a psych ward for ten days for observation."

She slowed her pace, slightly lowered her head, and kept scrubbing. "Sally, your brother was diagnosed as a paranoid schizophrenic."

I didn't know what to say. My welcome home —disheartening news of one of my siblings. Sad tears fell in my heart. Thomas had a label now to explain all his years of silence, anger, and talking to himself. He could finally get some help. I wondered about the rest of us.

"Sally Olivia, exactly what do you do?"

"For work? You know what I do; I'm a professional psychic medium."

"We thought for sure when you graduated, you'd make something of yourself. Become a doctor or even an actress for that matter, with all your speech and drama background."

Did she say actress? She was the one who said I didn't have a shot in hell of becoming an actress. I had never told her that I turned down the *Charlie's Angels* part.

She lit another cigarette, took a drag, and bitterly said, "But calling yourself a psychic and saying that you hear voices and talk to angels, you might be just like your brother."

"Mom, my life is good, and you're trying to tear it down. You don't waste any time … I'm successful, in love … with a very handsome, smart and talented … musician."

"Musician? Lord help you. You know how to pick them."

"Can I finish? I have a wonderful practice in Winter Park, and clients from all over the country come to see me. Did you forget I was on a special with a Beatle, graduated with honors, and left home early and have taken care of myself ever since? In a louder and more stern voice, I said, "So no, I'm not like Thomas!" I wanted to shout, "And I work for the NSA! Tell me how many lives you've saved lately?"

Instead, I calmed myself and turned my attention to Drifter, who looked like he was on his last breath from one too many cat fights. For my mother to criticize me was as natural for her as breathing. We could both be word-spinners, but her words came with an edge that made my heart want to quit and my body want to leave. I was hoping things had changed. They hadn't. I left the room and called Robert.

"Hi. I wanted to let you know I arrived."

"Hi babe, I'm glad you called. I miss you already. How's your mom?"

"Crazy," I said in a low voice, and added even in a lower voice, "Now I have a brother that's crazy, too."

"Did I hear you right? What did you say?"

"Nothing, I'll explain later. She's doing just fine. I miss you too. Are you playing anywhere tonight?"

"I'm playing at Xanadu's. I'm sitting in with the house band. Gotta run now and get ready to go downtown. Can we talk tomorrow?"

"Sure. Mom has a pre-surgery appointment. Afterward, we're going to lunch. Let's talk late afternoon or evening."

"Okay, hope all goes well. Bye, hon."

I hung up. I could picture Robert playing the drums, and his flock of admirers dancing in front of him. Was he in or out of the different-girl-every-night phase? *Trust him, Sally,* I said to myself, in the house that built mistrust.

THE NEXT DAY I made sure we drove different cars to Lexington. I met my parents in the lobby of St. Joseph Hospital. Her first words, "You're awful dressed-up."

"I was unsure where we were going for lunch." I had on a sleeveless white jumpsuit, black and white leather belt, and heels. "The Campbell House is nearby." It was one of my mother's favorite places to go.

"No, Sally! We can't afford that place. We're going to McDonald's. Are you joining us, or are you too good for that place?"

Day two of the barrage had begun. I thought, *If she's so close to dying, does she want McDonald's for her last meal, and when exactly did she become broke?* She could sell some of her precious quilts, or her two coveted Elvis tickets. She must have believed she was going to live at least until August 23rd to see him at Rupp Arena.

I went to McDonald's, ordered a fish sandwich, and sat and waited for them. They showed up and both ordered the same meal: Big Mac, fries, and a large coke. We all ate fast, in our usual style. Few words were spoken. My father went to the men's room before we left, and my mother looked coldly at me and said, "I can't wait until your life falls apart! You think you have it so good!"

I couldn't respond. I just looked at her with a sad, perplexing expression. *Boundaries,* I told myself, *remember my safety plan. Rule number one, vacate the scene.*

"Mom, I'm leaving. I'm not staying for your surgery. I came home to be with you, thinking it might be different this time. I know you might be on edge, but I'm not helping the situation by being here. I hope your surgery goes well. But this is a new low, even for you. What mother can't wait for their child's life to fall apart? Well, if my life falls apart, you'll be the first to know, so that you can be nominated for Mother of the Year."

I waited for Dad to come out and told him that I planned to return to Florida as soon as possible. I didn't need to explain why. He lived with her. My mother shouted as I walked toward my car, "Don't come to my funeral either."

I PHONED ROBERT. "Hey, I'm putting my evacuation plan in motion."

"Already. Good intentions went awry, I guess?"

"Yes. My mother is a walking volcano spewing lava everywhere. I've taken all that I can handle."

"Babe, it's been less than forty-eight hours."

"I know. Someday I'll share more with you. Then you may understand."

"I'm coming to Kentucky."

"No, please don't. Remember me and my sister's rule: If you want to keep a boyfriend, you don't bring him home to meet the Troubled Stones, especially the mother. If you want to ditch him, bring him home as quickly as possible … and Robert, I want to keep you."

"You're funny. I'm not coming to meet the family, but to explore a few ideas in Kentucky."

"Okay, but I'm still going to keep you away from the Stone clan. I'll be ready whenever you arrive. I'm going to try to talk privately to my father if given the chance, which is doubtful.

If you have any desire, we can visit some horse farms. Everything is Slewmania here, after Seattle Slew winning the Triple Crown."

"Babe, I'm more interested in my girl than the horses, but whatever you want."

"Well, the faster you arrive, the better, but there are no direct flights from Orlando to Lexington."

"Rosie, I'll handle it."

WITHIN RECORD TIME, Robert landed in Kentucky. I should've known he had enough clout to secure a government jet to transport him and would be driving a cool rental, too, a red Z28 Camaro.

"Let's create a pleasant memory of your visit. I've made reservations for us at the Duncan Tavern; it's a hotel in a quaint artist town called Hopewell. We can have a nice dinner, do some sight-seeing. Rosie, let's leave Betty Ann and family, Lang, Houseman, and Head, and the rest of the world behind." He forgot to mention the Roxys and the Bambees.

Of course, after a few glasses of wine, we didn't talk at all. Instead, we spent endless hours exploring each others' bodies. That evening I was better communicating with my body than with words. We slept peacefully, curled up with each other. Before leaving Hopewell, we drove around the town. We spotted this charming, unusual home tucked away on a hill and surrounded with luscious trees. It was only a half-mile from the square, but it seemed like it was out in the country. I had a vision as soon as my eyes saw it. We could be living in Kentucky, in that house, in that town, one day.

MY MOTHER NEVER MADE it to the August concert to see Elvis. She didn't die. Elvis did. He had a heart attack the week before the scheduled performance. My mom came out of surgery just fine and returned to her normal state.

Ticket to Ride

WITH KENTUCKY BEHIND US AND ROBERT BACK FROM A FIVE-DAY mission overseas, we were finally together in Winter Park. We were walking the grounds, hand in hand, with Fred and Ethyl when Robert said, "I'm leaving for a couple of months, headed to Russia."

"A couple of months. Why Russia?"

"Brezhnev has had two heart attacks and several small strokes. His days are numbered. He's a formidable adversary yet a stable force for peace with the US. I'll overtly work at the Moscow Embassy and try to feel out who has the power and position to succeed him. Unlike in our country, a new Russian leader has the ability to unilaterally change the course of international relationships. American treaties and relationships are scrutinized by Congress.

We need to prepare for the next regime."

Robert let go of my hand, reached down, and picked up a ball. As he threw it for Fred to retrieve, he said, "I also have a personal issue to resolve with a punk named Putin."

"What do you mean?"

"This guy has a vendetta against me. He's put out a contract to have me killed."

"Oh my God! Why?"

"I'm sure he suspects I'm responsible for several KGB deaths."

"Are you?"

"Maybe"

"What kind of answer is maybe?"

"It's the only answer I can give without violating my oath and agreements."

"Aren't we way past that? So you are accountable?"

"Yes. There's been no evidence or witnesses to anything I've done. But when I met Putin face to face during two summit meetings, he intently scanned me with his eyes and searched for anything to give him information."

"How can he know without facts?"

"Isn't it true you and I both know things without verification? He's smart and well-trained, young, hungry, aggressive, and willing to do anything to rise to the top. And in the spirit of full disclosure, a few years back, I was forced to kill his uncle."

"Forced?"

"I was on an assignment that should have been quick and clean, however, a KGB undercover agent got in the way. One thing led to another. It was either him or me. It turned out the agent was Putin's uncle."

"How did he figure that out?"

"Most likely it was simple math. I saw Putin when I was in Berlin; he saw me go into a building; his uncle went in after me. I came out. His uncle was dead. Case closed. This is the business all of us signed on for, even Putin."

By now I was holding back my feelings. I was beginning to feel vulnerable, when only moments before I felt elated. I continued to listen, hoping my fears would dissipate.

"Anyway, I'm sure I'll cross paths with him again, but for now … may I have a drumroll please … get ready to pack your bags, you're going to Egypt."

"What did you say? Egypt!"

"In a couple of months, the agency is sending you there for two weeks."

"What are you talking about?"

As we walked back to the house, each of us taking turns throwing the ball, Robert explained that since Tuck's death, he had been moved into the position of a senior covert agent. That put him in every strategy meeting, where he was consulted on entire operational missions. He was part of the overall planning, such as best personnel to engage, timing, strategy. He had wanted to tell me for some time about this multi-lateral play—him in Russia and me in Egypt.

When Egypt came up on the agenda, he presented me as the best psychic to go. ADCO Lang and DCO Stevens agreed, as long as the Spooks signed off on it. David and Gloria were in sync with his plan. The proposal entailed me vacationing as Sally Stone, a tourist. My goal would be to write a dossier and give us the pulse on what was going on politically: insight on the mood of the people, the politicians, and my visionary picture; size up Sadat's enemies, give the agency a read on Vice-President Mubarak and his political ties. The president of Quest Travel, Mohamed Razmy, a major player in the tourism industry, would arrange the introduction. He was a proponent of peace, like Sadat, and strove to establish good relations.

During my stay, Robert would be stationed two miles outside Cairo. There would be invisible support on the ground too. Egypt was unpredictable due to the recent peace accords with Israel. Disgruntled Arabs in the region had vowed to topple Sadat. If anything erupted, Robert wanted to be able to immediately transport me out. The best case scenario, he said, was that I would have a wonderful time without any problems. The country had solid laws and orderly communities throughout the area I would be in.

David and Gloria had other matters for me to attend to as well.

Robert hinted that I should picture myself floating down the Nile on an Egyptian sailboat, visiting temples along the way, and that Gloria had the particulars. Robert had noticed my affinity for Egypt when I moved in with all my books, and my Egyptian motif luggage and jewelry.

The plan sounded wonderful, except for someone wanting him dead. I was not crazy about the idea that he would be on one of his adversaries' turf for two months. Robert assured me that Putin would never make a move by himself. He was 5'7" and although he was in fine shape, he was no match for Robert. If he made a move and survived, he would have to live with being bested by an American spy. Either way, it was not the sort of thing a KGB agent desired on his resumé.

Robert told me to let him worry about the Russians, and to remember that when I talked with him at the embassy, the phones were more than likely monitored. I was to concentrate on learning as much as I could about the political scene in Egypt.

Fred and Ethyl followed us indoors. I was about to call Gloria when Robert suggested we have some afternoon delight. I could show him my gratitude for sending the Goddess to Egypt.

SEVERAL HOURS LATER, I was able to make that phone call. "Hi, Gloria! thank you! thank you!"

"You know about Egypt."

"Yes! I'm honored to be chosen to write the dossier and elated about sailing the Nile."

"I figured, what better place than Egypt to learn about healing and explore your potential? I found the Shamanic Egypt Tour and thought you'd fit in. You can write and experience the mystical land at the same time. I had a vision that you'll connect with the ancient spiritual forces and come back with a greater sense of purpose.

"David was supportive of the idea too. Between your visionary and writing abilities, he said your report may turn out to show the role we play in formulating trends and policies."

"If it's so important, why did they pick me instead of you?"

"Robert was the mastermind behind the trip, and he choreographed the timing. He knew I had several assignments in DC. I'm escorting the Egyptian ambassador to a White House dinner, and after that I'll assist the Deputy Secretary of State, Warren Christopher, at the Egyptian embassy daily while both countries hammer out new trade agreements."

Internally, I knew that Robert had indeed created this plan for me.

"I'll be getting a political read from this side of the ocean while you are doing the same on the other side. I left a folder for you in your office that'll help you organize your journey, a fourteen-day itinerary. Before I get off, I want to ask, how are you and Robert doing? Are you feeling better about the two of you?"

"Yes, I'm much better." *Especially after this afternoon.* "I still have trust issues. No doubt, he has a reputation and a past. The other day, a flight attendant came in my office for a reading. One of her questions had to do with a musician who worked at the Langford. This musician was her out-of-town lover. She wanted to know his status, whereabouts, anything I could get on him."

"I think I know where this is going … what did you say?"

"I asked her, 'Does his name happen to be Winston?' She said, 'Yes, yes, you're so good. What else do you get on him?'"

"Oh, Rose, how'd you handle that?"

"I said it would be best for the reading to come to a close. I told her I knew him personally and this was when reality crosses with the psychic world. It didn't help that she was his type—petite, shapely, and beautiful. I told her she probably wouldn't locate him on this trip. I only charged for half the time."

"You handled that fine. You can't blame your client for trying to find him, and you can't condemn Robert for his actions in the past. Since you two have been together, we don't have any sign that he's been unfaithful. If anything, he's tried to involve you more in his work. And you don't want to be like me, a thirty-something with no real love in your life."

"What about the new guy, Steven?"

"Yeah, I'm seeing him, but I'm unsure if it's going anywhere. Isn't it strange how we can see into the future of others, yet when it's up close and personal we can't always get an accurate read?"

"It's not fair, is it? I have a good feeling about this one. Thanks for helping me through my insecurities with Robert. You have a clearer picture than I do. I'd like to share a dream that I had last night. Do you have time? I know you have yoga class soon."

"Karate tonight but yes, tell me."

"I was lying in a stone box, a sarcophagus. I felt grounded to the earth's energies but simultaneously connected to the sky. I could hear and feel every heartbeat. I found myself in a vortex and transported to the edge of a remote cliff that overlooked a canyon and faced the setting sun. There was a voice, a calling, to trust and step off the bluff. I mustered the courage, and as I fell, I turned into a white dove. My wings stretched to catch me, and I found myself gliding and soaring above the land. I woke up to the sound of doves cooing outside my window. It took me a while to come back into my body. What do you think all that meant?"

"Egypt, my dear, the doorway to your future. Your time has come."

Back in the USSR

WHEN ROBERT ARRIVED AT THE US EMBASSY IN MOSCOW, HE WENT straight to Ambassador Thomas Watson's office. The secretary greeted him and notified the ambassador.

"Come in, who do I have the pleasure of meeting?"

"Mr. Watson, I'm Robert Sexton. I'm here as part of a routine information gathering for …"

"Okay son, you don't have to finish. It's best not to start our meeting with a lie.

"Have a seat. I know who you are and why you're here. CIA headquarters sent me a memo about you. No specifics."

Watson's office was exceedingly plush compared to most ambassadors. A massive, hand-carved desk covered most of a Persian rug. Beautiful sculptures and paintings dressed the room. Behind the desk was a picture of President Carter, standard fare for all embassies. There were also paintings from Picasso and Warhol. Attached to the Campbell's soup can image was a note. Robert didn't bother to read it.

"Robert, you can have complete access to my files."

"Thank you, sir."

"We don't stand on too much ceremony within our own ranks. You can call me Tom."

"With all due respect, sir, that might be difficult. After all, you're the CEO that made IBM the most powerful technology company on the planet. And you were the president of the Boy Scouts of America when I was a scout. I'm obliged to call you sir."

"If that makes you more comfortable. Now, what can I do for you?"

"I'd like to see your files regarding Brezhnev's medical history. Also, I need a list of safe houses throughout the city and nearby countryside."

"I anticipated that. I have them on my desk."

"One more request."

"What's that?"

"I'd like everything you have on Vladimir Putin."

"Now that I wasn't expecting. I know of the rising red star but was unaware that anyone from the States had him in their sights.

"Give me a minute." Mr. Watson beeped his secretary. "Gladys, get me everything we have on Vladimir Putin, please."

"By the way, sir, you were at Valley Forge when I played 'To the Colors' for President Johnson." Mr. Watson had aged gracefully from Robert's last recall. He was now in his mid-sixties, slightly bald, but still with a strong physique.

"It's a small world, isn't it?"

"Yes, sir."

"You must be skilled at what you do. You're not the first Eagle Scout to cross my path here in Moscow." He handed Robert a piece of paper. "Keep this with you. It contains two names that might be helpful. Mikhail Gorbachev, a member of the governing party Politburo, and Boris Yeltsin. They're friends, and I believe are the future of the USSR. God bless you, son, and good luck on whatever it is you're doing."

THE NEXT DAY, ROBERT took the Moscow Metro, Russia's showcase transportation, and stepped off at two kilometers east of Stalin Park. He headed to a small, modest house. The home was nearly empty inside, one bed and a small desk with short wave communications on it. The tiny refrigerator in the kitchen was stocked with essential foods and drinks. He waited to meet a familiar face, undercover NSA operative Ray White. Ray's military occupational specialty was electronic and computer surveillance.

Robert knew that the apartment building Putin lived in was being renovated. The entire structure was being retrofitted with the latest security and surveillance equipment. He also found out that the work was being outsourced to a Japanese firm, Yakushima Electric. In the spy game, favors were granted and saved up until needed, and Ray owed Robert a favor. Ray, whose mother was Japanese, had been passported as a Japanese citizen on more than one occasion. Robert arranged for him to be hired by Yakushima Electric under the name Rei Tanaka, upon registering with the Japanese Embassy.

After Ray had reported to the embassy, located in an upscale district of Moscow, he had received a Yakushima ID badge with his picture and thumb print on it. Then he went to meet Robert. He didn't know Roberts's plan, but it wasn't the first time he had worked in the dark.

"Good to see you, old friend."

"You too," said Ray. "What is it you wish for me to do?"

Robert told him about the plan. Alarms, cameras, audio, and lock installations were underway at the building Putin lived in. It was crucial that Ray convince the onsite general contractor that he was extremely skilled with the newest surveillance technologies. This should be easy, since Ray had more knowledge about this than any civilian installer.

The goal was for Ray to place three transmitters in Putin's

bedroom, kitchen, and living room, giving Robert full view and access to the apartment before the end of the day. Anticipating he would be searched, Ray hid the electronic devices he had smuggled into Russia in his work tool case, which had a false bottom.

After Ray had successfully placed the bugs, he asked if Robert was sure he wanted to surveil the home of a KGB agent. Robert told Ray that he was confronting Putin because the word was out that Putin had issued a hit on him.

"If you are going to confront Putin on his home field," said Ray, "Do you want me to stay and watch your six?" Robert thanked him for the offer but told him no.

"If you get caught bugging a KGB agent in Russia, what the hell is Lang going to say?"

"Not Lang's fight, this is personal. That's why I funded the mission myself. Besides, I have faith that you did a great job, there should be no hiccups. I have a driver that will safely get you to a small airport as soon as you're done and a crop duster that will fly you out. By the time Yakushima realizes that Tanaka is gone, I will have consummated my plan."

THE NEW ELECTRONIC BUGS allowed Robert to watch and hear Putin on a five-inch portable television. At 11:00 p.m., Putin took a shower and read before bed. His bedroom was cleverly laid out with lots of memorabilia. On one of the nightstands was a small turntable with American rock albums piled up on it. The Doors' *Waiting for the Sun* LP was lying on top. As Putin got into bed, he reached over and played "Hello, I Love You." Robert thought that was rather fortuitous.

Robert made his move at 3:00 a.m. His entrance was easy and effective, thanks to Ray, who had given him passwords to go through security undetected. In his adversary's bedroom, Robert pointed a gun at Putin's head. "Hello. Wake up, comrade."

"I see you've slipped through my security."

"I did that."

"You must have bugged my apartment."

"Yes, I did that."

"Are you planning to kill me?"

"Fair question, but unlike you, my friend, I don't kill unless it's the only option. I just want to talk."

"I don't know who you are or why you're here."

"Really, Vladdy, is that the way you're playing this? I had so much more respect for you. I thought you'd come clean."

"Okay, we play by your rules since you're holding the gun. You're Robert Sexton, CIA. You killed my uncle. You think I'm not professional. I know the rules, it's part of the game we play."

"Vlad, I'll give you that, you've done some decent research to figure that out. Not going to ask how, don't care. I know you're smart, but I'm holding the gun, so pay close attention, I don't want you to misinterpret my intentions. You put a contract out on me."

"Mr. Sexton, if I wanted you dead, you'd already be gone."

"Tough talk. I know you're behind it. You should call it off now before one of your comrades gets killed."

"Call off what? I know nothing."

"It's fortunate for you that I'm a man of peace."

"Now it's you, how you say, that spins the yarn?" said Vladimir. "You've killed many. You think we don't know about American involvement with Chernov, Gorky, and Gusev. Not to mention the poor children on the bus in Budapest."

At that, Robert nearly hit him across the face with the butt of the gun to leave a lasting reminder, but he stayed composed. He wondered how Putin knew about Budapest.

"Very low blow, even for you, but that's the way you play. Have a good night, Vlad."

Robert decided to hit him anyway, but not where it would show. With the heel of the gun, he hammered down on the man's rib cage. A bone cracked loud enough to be heard.

"Go ahead, kill me. See how Washington reacts to killing a KGB officer in Soviet Union. Your country is weak. If I kill you in your home, I am celebrated. So if you're not pulling trigger, please leave, so I can go back to sleep."

"Consider this a warning, anyone that comes at me will die, hard and fast, no mercy for an assassin. For the record, I didn't want to kill your uncle, he was going to kill me."

"We'll meet again, Sexton. Next time, per chance it may be on my terms. We'll see who holds gun then."

"I've said my piece. Any spilled blood will be on your head, not mine."

ROBERT CONTINUED TO WORK at the Moscow Embassy. Carissa Vankin, his Russian secretary, answered his phone with a thick accent: "American Consulate, how can I help you?" Carissa was a tall, sultry Russian woman with legs that went on forever and pouted thick lips that were always adorned with ruby red lipstick. She was small-waisted, with 36C breasts that she scarcely covered. The old Robert would've snatched her up in a New York minute, but he was committed to Rose and barely noticed Carissa. This seemed to make Carissa even more flirtatious.

"I'd like to speak with Robert Sexton," said the caller.

"Who's calling?"

"Rose Casallie."

"You're with who?"

"I'm with Robert Sexton. We went through this the last time I called."

"Can I tell him what this is about?"

"No, I'd rather tell him myself."

"Just a minute, I'll see if he's available."

"Mr. Sexton, I have Rose Casallie on the line. Do you want me to tell her that you're busy?"

"No, put her through."

"Hey, Rosie, miss me?"

"Yes, I miss you. I never thought the Russian chick would put me through to you. Each time she acts like she doesn't remember who I am."

"I know what you're saying, babe, but I'm not the one that placed her here. How about that technology? I'm halfway around the world, and it sounds like you're next door.

"I wish. I've been uneasy ever since you told me about the Putin thing."

"Darling, you know how much I admire him."

"Yes, exactly, that's what I meant."

"Even though we're talking on an American embassy line, we know it's not cleared. So say hello to Russia, they're always listening. Are you excited about your vacation? I wish I could join you, but the ambassador has this crazy idea that we're supposed to show up for work. Carissa says I need to run; we have a reception to attend. Which I might add will be mundane and boring. I'm such a diplomat."

"Really, is she intervening again?"

"I'll call you next week before you travel. Don't let Rissa upset you. Stop and remember I love you. You're going to Egypt."

Walk Like an Egyptian

THE DAY CAME FOR MY PILGRIMAGE TO EGYPT. I ARRIVED AT JFK Airport and recognized other fellow travelers by the purple Shamanic Egypt Tour identification tags that we had received with the itinerary. We boarded Egypt Air in the early evening and arrived at the Cairo airport at noon. We disembarked into glaring heat and were taken by bus to the terminal. Fourteen travelers from around the world came together. My Egyptian luggage, which was finally making a proper trip, was the only luggage in the group that didn't arrive. Thankfully, I had carried an overnight bag with toiletries and an extra change of clothes. There were no more flights for the day, so I hoped my bags would come before we flew to Luxor, the earliest capital of Egypt.

We moved through customs and immigration with little difficulty, getting visas and Egyptian pounds in exchange for dollars. Travel-weary, I noticed an abundance of stern and serious military personnel throughout the tattered, worn airport. I felt safe knowing Robert was close by. I was wearing a topaz pendant that he had given me before the trip. Inside it was a device to track my steps on the sacred land.

Quest Travel was tracking down my suitcases, but I was sure that Robert was already on it. I quickly learned Egyptian public bathrooms required payment in exchange for toilet paper. If we wanted liquor during the upcoming sail, we had to buy it immediately at the duty-free store. Following that notice, a small stampede preceded as about half the group went to secure selected wines and spirits. We then left by bus for our accommodations.

After leaving the long traffic jams in Cairo, we traveled to Giza. The closer we got to Giza; the traffic began to snarl again. We were enveloped in a symphony of car horns and other harsh sounds of the streets. No one obeyed the lane markers. There were no traffic lights but plenty of camels, donkeys, and horses in the streets, adding chaos.

The pyramids rose on the smog-filled horizon and reminded us that we were in a three-thousand-year-old, or more, city—the land of the pharaohs. We arrived in Giza at the luxurious Mena House Oberoi, a hotel frequented by celebrities and politicians. A year before, Egyptian and Israeli officials had convened in that same hotel in a quest for a peace settlement. The results of that conference had led to the Camp David Accords, which restored Egypt's sovereignty over the Sinai Peninsula and cemented a peace agreement between the two countries.

I was paired to share a room with Ginelle Corbit, a Romanian gymnast. She had arrived two days earlier and was in the room when I entered. It was her second visit to Egypt, and she had come early to have more time in Giza. Our windows opened on a direct view of the majestic Great Pyramid. As soon as Ginelle learned of my lost belongings, she kindly offered to share her clothes until mine appeared. At 5'4", she was a couple of inches shorter than I and weighed about a hundred-and-eight pounds with no body fat, petite but all muscle.

After a few hours of rest, we all met in the tour leader's room for an opening circle. Going around the room, we introduced ourselves and spoke our intentions for coming to Egypt. We each drew a tarot card from the Egyptian Anubis deck. I secretly drew two, one for Rose Casallie and the other for Sally Stone.

The card for Rose was Maat, a goddess personified as a female wearing a tall feather on her head; Maat represented the ancient Egyptian concept for truth, justice, and cosmic order. It was the king's duty to uphold Maat for the entire country, so much so that the value and legitimacy of the king's reign depended upon how well he maintained Maat. I thought the card fitting for my assignment, since I was there to read the political pulse of the people and the leaders, the Maat of Sadat and Mubarak. In shamanic astrology, Maat represented Libra. I thought of Robert, a Libra, and indeed a warrior for the American Maat.

As Sally Stone on the trip, I shared my second card. I had drawn Bast, half-cat and half-human. It meant holy longing and desire and represented my sign in Scorpio. My longing and desire were to use my gifts for the highest good, doing God's will. And I still desired to understand the true meaning of home and family. Was it with the NSA, in Kentucky, Robert, or my pilgrimage to Egypt?

My roommate pulled the card Set. In the deck, each archetype has a powerful role, and Set performs his purpose by opening people to their dark and shadow side, often personifying turmoil and confusion. Perhaps by the end of the trip we'd all understand our deities and their meaning even more. For now, Ginelle was my best ally, especially since she had packed extra clothes and items, a perfect match for my predicament.

After introductions, we had a welcome dinner in the formal restaurant, where I met Mohamed and his assistant Emil Carakus. Mohamed was a big, gregarious man with a full face, smooth olive skin, heavy-lidded eyes, and jet-black hair that had a white streak at the front. He was dressed in an Armani suit and spoke elegantly. Seated to the right of him at dinner, I had a close view of his marketing and hospitality skills. He invited me to have breakfast with him on our second day in Giza. I knew he was my connection to meet influential political leaders but felt confident he only knew me as Sally Stone, an American tourist with no political agenda.

We rose early the next morning for a private sunrise visit to the Giza Plateau, my first connection to that ancient ground. It was breathtaking as we paid our respects to the Sphinx, the guardian of the Mysteries, who sees our incarnations and keeps the Hall of Records where our stories are kept. Nestled between the Sphinx's paws, I reiterated my sacred intentions and prayed: "I align my will with the will of the Divine, and here I am. I'll do what you ask of me, whatever that may be."

We visited the oldest pyramid, the Step Pyramid of Djoser, which houses the sanctuary of sound and healing. This magnificent site included Old Kingdom tombs, among them those holding the earliest known hieroglyphs. Our visit inside the Great Pyramid was scheduled for our last night.

The afternoon was free, and Ginelle offered to accompany me to the Khan bazaar. While the rest of the travelers were busy looking for papyruses, jewelry, scarves, and Egyptian souvenirs, we searched out clothing in case my luggage never arrived. The atmosphere at this traditional market, with the labyrinthine layout of the surrounding streets, gave me a glimpse into the medieval period. We spotted security guards at every turn, and we especially couldn't ignore the large shadow that accompanied us our entire shopping trip, a tall and broad-shouldered young guy wearing a heavy suit jacket to hide the automatic pistol that he carried. Ginelle tried to persuade the guard to go away, telling him that she knew her way around. He was determined to stay with us as we meandered through the narrow streets among textiles and spices and men sitting on steps smoking hookahs. I assumed Robert had arranged for the guard to escort us, an extra measure to the tracking pendant.

The next morning, I had breakfast with Mohamed and other dignitaries in a reserved room, my first opportunity to meet and psychically read some political faces. I was the only one in our group to attend. Ginelle saw me leave with Mohamed, and on return she asked how that had transpired. I said that Mohamed had enlisted me to participate in a photo op with some dignitaries who took every opportunity to include attractive American women in photos to increase the tourist industry as well as the politician's reputation. She seemed to buy that, and I chose to keep the details private, particularly my meeting with the vice-president, Hosni Mubarak.

The flamboyant Mubarak had addressed me with a smile and a small gracious bow of the head. As his photographer snapped shots, I could sense Mubarak's power and control. As soon as we shook hands, I felt his energy: unsettling, dark, and heavy, and in contrast to his appearance. I received a strong psychic hit that this man wasn't who he appeared to be. He had two personalities: one that he showed America, and one for the Arab world. Within a couple of minutes, I saw something like a screen show in my head. I didn't know when it would happen, but I saw Mubarak replace Sadat as the leader of the country and counteract all the progress that Sadat had done for peace, free and fair elections, and for Egyptian women by bringing them into the twentieth century. More importantly, I saw renewed relations with Russia. I made mental notes so I'd remember my visions and impressions when writing the dossier.

After breakfast, I joined the group on the tour bus to visit the Egyptian Museum of Cairo. When we arrived, we were given preferential treatment as we went through security. Once again, the security were armed with much firepower. The museum held an astounding collection of Egyptian antiquities. There were over 100,000 artifacts, including those from the tomb of Tutankhamun.

Time was too short to view the spiritual legacy of the numerous priests, kings, queens, scribes, and healers. In the museum, it felt like a hundred radio frequencies were broadcasting simultaneously to the receiver in my head. I experienced psychic anxiety, being close to so many displaced statues that had been seized from their consecrated homes and brought to the museum without regard for the energy that resided within them. The chatter of many foreign dialects didn't help either. I saw numerous Russian-speaking men, which surprised me, as my research had told me Sadat had deported most of the Russians. I did my best to stay grounded and centered amid the spiritual and diplomatic forces of Egypt.

Do You Believe in Magic

MY BAGS DID NOT ARRIVE BEFORE WE BOARDED THE FLIGHT TO Luxor. I had to depend on Ginelle's generosity until we had another market opportunity. As soon as we landed in Luxor, we were taken by bus, then by water taxi, to our beautiful private dahabeeyah, a sailing boat like those that had traditionally carried Egyptian royalty up and down the Nile. Her name was *Afandina* and she had a steel hull and construction to the finest maritime specifications. The interior had the feel of an English pub with plank wood flooring. The smiling crew greeted us with a refreshing drink of lemon and a wet washcloth to wipe the soils of our travel.

After taking in the splendor on the main deck, we ventured to the lower level to find our quarters. Ginelle and I called Cabin Five ours for the duration. It had twin beds with a night table between, and for the next nine days it was our home on the Nile. Our days often began visiting a temple to watch the sun rise and ended with sunset. In between, there was plenty of time to relax, write, reflect, and drift on the boat.

In Luxor, we toured Karnak, one of the largest and most magnificent worship complexes in the world. Twin obelisks dominated the temple's skyline and guarded the gates. Emil, a master storyteller, led us around the maze and translated the hieroglyphs. He shared different stories of the creation of light as the sunlight passed from pillar to pillar through the grand hall. One of the temple's attendants got my attention and without words motioned me to enter a small chapel outside the main hall. I hesitated briefly then followed him. The chapel was dedicated to Sekhmet, lion-headed goddess of compassion and courage. She was associated with feminine fires and was a healer known for her magic and ability to hunt down an imbalance at its origin. She was also the guardian of Maat, goddess of justice, balance, and truth. This statue of Sekhmet contrasted greatly to those I had seen in the museum because it was still whole and in its original place, where it had stood for thousands of years.

When I approached Sekhmet, her power amplified. Her intense eyes looked right through me, and I laughed involuntarily out of recognition, not disrespect. I heard her speak by thought: *Where have you been? I've been waiting for you. We both know what is going on. We have an ancient history together. Time has come to recognize your fierceness, your compassion, your healing abilities. Be who you are, a healer, and receive the gift of courage to be your authentic self.* It was in the same tone a general would use to say, "At ease, soldier."

After receiving the lioness' message, I bowed my head then thanked and tipped the guard for taking me to an area where others weren't allowed. As I left, I took time to touch the ancient, sacred sycamore tree at the entrance to the sanctuary, Hathor's tree of healing.

I determined that each temple had two kinds of protection: the Tourist Police and the Temple Guards. The policemen wore uniforms with guns and holsters, boots, and berets, and the other guards wore white scarves around their heads like turbans and plain blue jellabiyas. A jellabiya is a garment with long sleeves, open at the neck, that comes to the ground. When worn by women, it can be ornate and embroidered; the man's form is normally of plain sheeting. The guards carried machine guns. In some temples, they wore their arms over their jellabiyas and in others underneath their robes. Either way, they were prepared to shoot if something criminal happened.

When I returned to the group, Emil was still telling stories. I hurriedly made notes of my experience in my journal. Flashbacks of Gloria came to mind: her telling me early on how she believed I was a healer, and what better place to learn about healing than Egypt. And here I stood, absorbing the ancient energies ... energetically, spiritually, and mentally. Repeated themes and images kept appearing—Maat and justice, light and dark, yin and yang, healer and warrior.

In the evening, we visited the lighted Luxor Temple, where we invited the Divine into our human vessels as we walked through the avenue of sphinxes. The eyes of those human-headed lions seemed to watch our every step and ask, "Are you ready to offer everything to the Creator Spirit and become a pure and worthy vessel to contain the spiritual light?" My hands heated up as soon as I asked the Creator that I become a celestial vessel for goodness and healing. The pulsating and burning sensations subsided after I placed my hands on my chest. I heard the voice of an angel: *Sally, carry your temple with you. You never walk alone.* Thoughts danced through my mind while vibrations danced in my body. I wondered if maybe the home I had been searching for was within my own container. Thoughts of my mother were continents away. Thoughts of Robert were close to my heart. Thoughts of God were everywhere.

Emil, who noticed that everyone in the temples gave me special attention, bowed to me like royalty. When he had the chance, he pulled me aside and said, "You must have powers you're unaware of. You're being recognized by the guards, the police, the women, the

Egyptian children, and by the temples themselves. I need to bring you to Sabria, the oldest, wisest healer and seer in Egypt, maybe in the entire world. I'll try to make that happen for you."

That evening I had a dream that I was a shaman who worked her magic as an alchemist, able to transform the dark and light energies of opposites into something sacred. A Medicine Woman.

As we continued to sail, Robert the Hawk traveled with us every bit of the Nile. Appropriately, a hawk hovered above our boat as we moved to the Temple of Horus, one of the most beautiful preserved temples in Egypt. Horus is depicted as a hawk-headed man wearing a double crown with the sun disk on it.

Emil entertained us with the stories carved on the walls. Here we learned about the triumph of Horus: the story of Isis birthing Horus, Horus fighting Set, Horus and Set's shape-shifting ability, and lastly the defeat of Set by Horus. The story encouraged us to seek our own empowerment by working to balance the lunar and solar energies inside of us—the feminine and masculine—and like a hawk, awaken our intuitive centers to experience a higher perspective.

Side chambers of Horus' temple showed the complexity of the god's rites, which used a healing chamber, a perfumery, and a singer's room. Each chamber brought up visions for me. In the music room, I remembered the story Robert had told me about shape-shifting into a hawk so he could see approaching danger. Horus, husband of the goddess Hathor, became patron of the pharaohs and was called the son of truth, signifying his role as a vital upholder of Maat.

Emil arranged for me to meet Sabria in Dendera at the temple dedicated to Hathor, the goddess of love and joy. To start our tour, Emil guided us to a room with one of the world's earliest zodiacs on the ceiling. It was a replica, but still amazing to see. The original sits in the Louvre in Paris. I thought of my great aunt and how she would have loved to have seen it. On the way out, Emil directed us to an underground crypt at the rear. Those who weren't claustrophobic descended into the ground where we found ourselves in a shaft barely large enough for two people to pass each other. Around the corner were hieroglyphs of the story of creation, before and after. One wall depicted two cobras woven around a staff. The snakes represented energy and alluded to the higher consciousness and vibration of energy. I was the first one to slither into the passageway to the crypt, and to slither my way out.

Upon my exit, a guard greeted me, an American of Egyptian descent. He led me into an area called Hathor's Music and Jubilation Room. Stairs, small and plentiful, ascended to a balcony where you could look out an open window and see the vast land. As I reached the last step, I saw an ancient-looking woman seated on a stone bench. Behind her was a wall of hieroglyphics of the goddess Hathor and scenes of singers, musicians, dancers, all intoxicated with wine and joy.

I sat beside her. Her thin, wrinkled, warm hands touched my forehead briefly, before gently holding both of my own. She whispered, "I'm Sabria, and I've seen into your soul and into your crystal blue eyes. You are a healer of great magnitude. You will heal yourself and others. You will master the anechoic reception chamber, ARC healing, and teach it to others. You're going to—"

"I don't understand, I'm just learning about healing. I don't know anything about—"

"Don't worry, my child, you're young, and healing is something you can't learn at once. It comes continually throughout your life and takes years to master. You're a vessel for higher powers. Being a vessel is complex, it's more than the laying-on of hands. It's thought-healing too. You'll learn to concentrate, meditate, channel your thoughts, raise your vibration, and direct the astral forces. As you become, you lose yourself, and just be."

"I'm more lost than ever."

"Child, to lose your way is to arrive. Voices from enlightened ancestors will remind you of the power of the heart and call you to bring their consciousness into the present to help you remember your true nature as a sacred human with a soul purpose.

"You will also visit the Great Pyramid before you return home. You will have an invitation to enter the sarcophagus in the King's Chamber. It'll be your initiation in the chamber that will directly connect you to the ARC. Here you will unite your life story with the story of those who have come before you and those who'll come after you, as you embrace your transformation."

"I have dreamed of lying in an ancient stone box."

"I know, my dear, another step in raising your consciousness and vibration. You will also connect with saints, angels, archangels, ascended masters, the Egyptian *neteru*, and ..."

She reached beside her and picked up an instrument, twelve inches long and four inches wide, that consisted of a handle surmounted by a simple metal hoop frame that held small rings and bells. She shook it for me to hear the sound, and then placed it in my hands. "It's an ancient type of musical rattle called a sistrum." The shape was similar to its equivalent, an ankh, representing the sign of life.

"The symbolic value of the sistrum far exceeds its musical potential. It's used to evoke protection, divine blessing, and rebirth. I have placed the Living Sea Scrolls inside the sistrum's handle for safe keeping. My child, keep these sacred scrolls that hold the ARC magic in this secret and safe container. Open them when the time and place is right. Be careful not to speak about them until you've mastered the meaning."

"How will I know when the time and place are right?"

"Child, the ARC finds you in divine time. Know this: the healer and the wounded must be of pure heart for the restorative powers of the universe to work."

I lost track of time and had no recollection of how long I was with Sabria, when we left the balcony or temple, or when I placed the sistrum in my handbag. My next memory was being on a water taxi heading back for another night's sleep on the *Afandina*.

Ginelle expressed concern when I arrived in the room. Emil had told the group that I had become claustrophobic and overheated after exiting the underground passageway and had to be escorted away.

"You look different. I can't put my finger on it." Ginelle stepped further back from me and took a deeper look. "I thought you'd be exhausted; instead you look refreshed and extremely peaceful. You're almost glowing. What did they give you?"

I smiled and said, "Just water and music."

Wind Beneath My Wings

the sun on the deck, a yacht with the name *Yankee* passed by. I couldn't believe it. Robert was traveling with me whether he knew it or not. The crew told us that the boat was owned by a married couple who took it on notable sailing trips all around the world, and the Nile was their current expedition.

Ginelle saw my surprised expression and I offered an explanation. "Winston, my boyfriend, is a huge Yankees fan. It's strange to be reminded of him here on the Nile."

"What does Yankee mean?" she asked.

"In World War I, the Brits called American soldiers Yankees. It's also the name of a baseball team that Winston almost played for."

"Do you have a picture of him?"

I had my journal with me, and I pulled out a photo of Robert for her to see. She looked at it intently. I understood why. The photo showed him with long hair and beard, wearing only shorts, and flexing his tan arm muscles and baring his defined abs. When she returned the picture, she asked, "What does your boyfriend do? He's in incredible shape, looks like a gymnast or martial artist?"

"He's a ... musician. He could've been a baseball player because of his speed but—"

"A musician. I've never seen musicians in that kind of shape. What instrument does he play?"

"He plays mostly piano and guitar."

"Where does he play, Florida?"

"He plays all over but is often a regular in Winter Park or Orlando, sometimes solo, sometimes as a backup with traveling bands."

"Orlando? I'll be there next week. As soon as I return to Romania, I leave again."

"Why Orlando?"

"I'm scheduled to attend several events at the Pan American preliminaries. I'm sure I'll be jet-lagged. My husband isn't crazy about it either, but he's used to my traveling. How strange is it that I'll be visiting where you live?"

"Let's try to get together. We live only twenty minutes away from Orlando, and you're welcome to stay with us. I'm not sure if Winston will be there, his schedule is subject to changes."

"No, I have to stay with my group; my visa requires it. But we'll make it work. I love music, so if Winston is playing, perhaps I could meet him too, and have some American fun."

"And if your luggage doesn't arrive, you can count on me returning the favor of clothing you."

THE TIME CAME, and we said farewell to our beloved *Afandina*. We took an early flight to Cairo. Due to Ginelle's gymnastic schedule, she had to depart straight from Cairo to Romania and missed the King's Chamber visit in the Great Pyramid. We said our goodbyes and agreed to see each other when she arrived in the US. I had the Mena House hotel room to myself. I turned my attention to completing the dossier while events were still fresh in my mind.

My conclusion was that Sadat stood as a true friend of the US and

Israel. Sadat had hidden enemies near him, Mubarak being one. Sadat had dismissed allegations that the current rioting had been induced by domestic issues, believing the Soviet Union had recruited its regional allies in Libya and Syria to cause an uprising that would eventually force him out of power. I felt the Russians were starting to make a stronger presence. My prediction was that Sadat would be assassinated, Mubarak would become the new leader, and the Russian consulate would reopen. There would be no more free elections. Mubarak would become a dictator with the backing of the Russians, the same Russians that Sadat had thrown out, saying they were no friends to the Arabs.

I put the dossier aside and tried to prepare for my upcoming visit to the Great Pyramid. The Living Sea Scrolls that Sabria had given me would have to wait until I found a sacred and tranquil space. I placed a handwoven silk cloth around the sistrum and papyruses and put them away.

Usually, thousands of people tour the Giza plateau every day, and only a hundred and fifty are allowed into the pyramid, waiting in line up to three hours in the hot sun to go inside for just a few minutes to see a chamber containing a stone box. Our group had special privileges, thanks to Mohamed's efforts. We were able to go after-hours, with no tourists, and spend some time in the King's Chamber. To enter, one must crawl, squat, or bow low, no easy task for the few in the group who had bad knees or backs. Once through this long flight of steep stairs, we came into a high-chambered ceiling that relieved any feelings of claustrophobia. We proceeded to the King's Chamber. Above our heads hung granite slabs weighing fifty tons each. A stone sarcophagus carved from a single block of granite sat at the opposite end of the room.

Each of us had the opportunity to lie in the sarcophagus for a couple of minutes. I was the last. It was similar to what I had described to Gloria about my dream. I invoked all the directions and invited all the spirits, beings, and archangels as my bare feet touched this ancient stone. I opened myself to the universal field of energy and a force took over. My body began to shake. My conscious awareness was drawn away from my body and seemed to travel upward, through the Pyramid's apex. There was a sense of movement, swift and causing momentary vertigo. The sound of my heartbeat lifted the veil and opened my eyes to the astral spheres. I saw a vision, an arc of light and vibration moving from my electromagnetic field and body directly to a Divine source. A vessel of God. I went into the King's Chamber with one vibration and departed with a different frequency. I knew my spirit had been aligned with Holy light and sound.

OUR TRIP ENDED WITH a closing dinner in the formal dining room. Upon entry, I heard piano music playing. I instantly thought of Robert. I didn't know if I was still in the astral plane of consciousness or not, because now I heard Robert's voice. I looked around, and to my astonishment there he sat, dressed in Egyptian attire, playing the piano and singing. It took everything I had to remain calm and not look at him. I thought, *How does he do the things he does?* The night ended with Mohamed saying his goodbyes to each of us. At the table, we all held hands in a circle and sang John Lennon's "Imagine" while Robert played.

When the song ended, we all said our *adieus* as Robert disappeared into the night.

"Rose," whispered Emil. "I'm with Robert."

"Ode to Joy," I said.

"Ludwig Beethoven." Code word confirmed.

"He wanted me to tell you Horus the Hawk will be waiting for his goddess Hathor when she arrives back in the States."

Lyin' Eyes

 Airport. I had to wait several hours for my military transport back to Meade. I reread my dossier, then faxed it to headquarters. By the time I landed in Maryland and shuffled back to the base, David had already read my Egyptian profile.

"Rose, you managed to surpass my expectations. This dossier may help us in the future if we ever need to defend the importance of our department." David placed the folder on his desk. "In addition to your assignment, I understand you had some spiritual experiences as well."

David kept in-depth files on each of us. They served as documentation of our individual growth and represented his thirty years' involvement with the agency. He was eyeing retirement and wanted to make sure that the next DOS was up to speed on his unit if he should leave.

"Watching the professional and personal growth of my team is truly rewarding for me. You've earned a few weeks off, so what are your plans?"

"I haven't seen Robert in eight weeks, except for his surprise appearance at the closing ceremony. So I'm heading home as soon as you dismiss me."

The mention of Robert always intrigued David. He believed that

Robert should've been part of the paranormal division.

"He does have a way of appearing and disappearing. You guys enjoy your R and R. See you in a couple of weeks."

"By the way, my roommate in Egypt, Ginelle Corbit, is visiting me in the next couple of days. She's a Romanian gymnast attending the Pan Am Games. Just giving you a heads-up, since Romania has an off-and-on-again relationship with the Soviet Union."

"I appreciate the info, say hi to Robert, and you're dismissed. Have fun."

ROBERT GREETED ME at the Orlando airport with an extra-long kiss and tight embrace. It felt so good to be in his arms and for both of us to be back together. Home, safe.

"You look freaking amazing, Sally Rose." *Freaking amazing!* "I missed you more than you could know." After the long, tedious flights, I knew I looked tired and worn out, but I had gotten used to Robert's upbeat homecomings.

"I missed you too."

"It feels like I haven't held you in my arms for a year. I can't wait to get you home. Let me escort the goddess to her palace." His car was parked right out outside baggage claim. Today he was behind the wheel of his red 1978 BMW M1. He opened the passenger door. "Was Egypt everything you had hoped for?"

"Yes, and more. Part of me is still on the Nile. Seeing you on our last night was incredible, and yet it was so difficult to act like you were invisible. There's so much to share with you."

"I can't wait to hear all about it. I had a feeling Egypt would be a profound experience.

"Before I forget," Robert reached over and patted my thigh. "Your mom called yesterday. I guess you must have told her you were going to Egypt?"

"I did. Said I was going on a spiritual retreat."

"She started crying, said you were in dangerous land and may not return and how much she loved you."

"What else did my mother have to say?"

"She wants you to come home and put your name on the items you want after she dies. Like her quilts. Mentioned that everyone wants the lazy Susie table. She's asking your brothers and sister to do the same."

"Is she dying again?"

"I don't know, you know your mom."

"How about she first returns the things she stole from me?" I thought I just said it under my breath, but obviously I didn't because Robert said, "What are you talking about?"

I briefly told Robert the aftermath of the loose marble story. I was too tired to go into much detail. I explained to Robert that she had evicted me from the apartment behind the house. But before I had time to move, my mother had used her key and taken my favorite possessions. The angel prints that had hung over my bed as a child, a vase that was my great grandmother's, and the quilt she had given to me.

For my high school graduation, I was allowed to choose one quilt out of my mother's collection. She had over three hundred. Most were old and handmade, though a few were new and cheap. One hundred had to be in shades of blue. Her obsession had started with a lifetime feud with her mother. My mother was always bitter that my grandmother never gave her some quilts that she had promised her. So my mother went on a crusade to collect as many as possible.

I had picked my favorite—a baby blue and white one, handmade by Sadie. That was the one she stole, and when I asked for it back, her reply was, "You'll get it, over my dead body."

"So, no," I concluded. "I'm not going home to put my name on anything. Once she knows I like something, she either takes it away or tears it down."

"Honey, your family stories sure are strange. Babe, before I could get off the phone, she invited me to come with you on your next visit. Something about filling me in on the real Sally Olivia."

"Not happening."

"Don't shoot the messenger. Grab that device in the back seat."

"What is it? It's heavy." I could see the formation of what appeared as dial buttons, but it felt like a handheld weapon.

"It's a new devise that the DOD is experimenting with. It's called a cellular phone."

"Kind of cumbersome."

"We each have our own. Now there's instant communication when necessary."

"I'm not sure if my handbag is big enough to conceal it."

"Speaking of your handbag … we're still trying to locate your missing luggage. How did you manage without it? Are you wearing one of your market finds?"

"Yes, but my roommate Ginelle was a lifesaver. We were close in size; she graciously shared her clothes. Ironically, she's arriving in Orlando tomorrow, and we plan to meet."

"What's she doing here?

"She's a former gold medalist in the last Olympics. She's attending the Pan Am Games as an observer with the Romanian Olympic team. I'd love for you to meet her. I showed her your picture and—"

"Whoa! I thought we didn't do that kind of thing. She could've recognized me at the final farewell."

"She wasn't at the closing ceremony; she left a day early. I barely recognized you. You looked more Egyptian than some Egyptians. Seeing the *Yankee* yacht was the catalyst to showing her the photo. You're right, though, I shouldn't have. My energies were so scattered."

"Yeah, I heard about the boat. No, I didn't plan for that to happen, but it was kind of cool that it did."

"Will you be free tomorrow tonight? Ginelle and I are having dinner. I do want to show you off."

"I have a gig, but I can join you at the Langford while you girls have a drink. I'm playing at Buena Vista's Dutch Inn Lounge. Come over after dinner, if you wish."

"My phone is ringing. Who can that be? I don't even know the number to that big thing. Surely you didn't give my number to my mother!"

"No, of course not. Answer it. Must be someone from the agency. We're the only people who currently have this device."

"Hello."

"Hi, Rose."

"Hi, Gloria.

"Welcome home! We have a new way to communicate now. Listen, I'm headed to Orlando tomorrow, and I can't wait to see you and hear more about your trip. Plus I have some news of my own."

"Oh my God, did Steven propose?"

"Yes! I'll fill you in tomorrow with the details. I want to hear about your real Egyptian experience, not just what was in the dossier. I'll catch up with you tomorrow. Can't wait to see you. Bye."

AS SOON AS WE pulled into our drive, I heard the dogs barking. They were so excited to see me, they nearly knocked me to the ground. I put down my bags and hugged both of them as they licked my face. Ethyl was beginning to gray, but she carried on like a new pup. Robert picked me up and carried me in like a bride. We were both so happy to be home. No Rissa, Putin, Betty Ann, or anybody else, tonight belonged to us.

Robert drew me a hot bath, lit some candles, and opened a bottle of cabernet.

THE NEXT DAY I was still on an Egyptian and lover's high. I didn't want to get out of bed, but I did. Between Robert, the dogs, and the bird aviary, I was becoming more grounded being back in the US.

I called my mother to let her know I had returned safely from my trip. I also let her know I had no plans to come to Kentucky any time soon. Her tone morphed into a slightly angry one and out of context with our conversation she said, "Sally, are you going to come to my funeral? I need to know!"

"When is it?" I said, in a matter-of-fact way.

There was no sound on the other end of the phone. She did not like my dry humor. It was my only option, as I was in no mood for her drama or manipulative tactics. I tried to take the higher road and change the subject.

The day seemed to pass far too quickly before it was time to meet up with Ginelle.

Robert and I had just sat down at the Langford when she entered the restaurant. Her black hair was styled to perfection. She wore a sleek, sexy white dress, showing off her muscular and toned figure that moved with precision atop four-inch stiletto heels. I almost didn't recognize her. Heads turned as she confidently promenaded over to our table. We gave each other a kiss and a big hug.

"So, you must be Winston. Sally told me so much about you, I feel as though I know the Yankee Hawk."

"Nice to meet you, Ginelle. Welcome to our part of the world. Where are you staying?"

"Park Plaza."

"Oh, right here in Winter Park." Winston said.

"Yes, the teams are doing warmups at Rollins College."

"I shoot around for fun with the basketball team at the college. Sally has told me how much you helped her out in Egypt. I thank you for being there for her."

"Winston is playing at the Dutch Inn at Disney tonight. He has to leave shortly. We can stay here and catch up and visit him later. I'll tell you about what you missed on the last night."

"Waiter, a bottle of your best cabernet for these two girls, please. Silver Oak, if you have it. And a ginger ale for me. Sally told me that good red wine was scarce on the Nile."

"Yes, it was. I have to go light on the wine tonight, but thank you for your selection. And one glass won't hurt."

"Cork what you don't drink." Winston said.

He stood from the table, shook Ginelle's hand, then leaned in and kissed me goodbye. "Bye, babe, see you in a couple of hours. We're playing from ten to one."

"We'll try to be there before the last set. Ginelle has been wanting to hear American music."

Ginelle smiled softly and said, "You seem like a very happy couple."

No sooner had Robert left then Gloria showed up at our table.

"I can't believe it. How'd you know I'd be at the Langford?"

"Maybe because every time I visit you and Winston we eat at the Langford."

"Ginelle, this is my friend, Gloria. She's a boutique buyer, always on the road. I mean in the air, in and out of the garment district. And Gloria, this is the girl I told you about from the trip."

"Nice to meet you."

"Likewise."

"I only have a couple of hours," Gloria replied. "Early plane to catch in the morning. But yes, Steven surprised me while you were gone." Gloria flashed her left hand. Her perfectly manicured red polish nails showed off the sparkling diamond.

"I love the setting, beautiful." Ginelle said.

"Thank you."

Gloria turned to me. "I'd like you to be my maid of honor."

"Yes, of course, I'd be honored. I'm so happy for you."

Throughout dinner, we vacillated back and forth from tales about Egypt to wedding preparation. With dinner almost over and the wine nearly gone, Ginelle said, "I have an idea, why don't I take a taxi to see Winston perform? You two have so much to talk about. We can catch up tomorrow. I'm going to be here all week. You two need to talk about wedding plans. You hang with her; I'll go listen to some rock and roll."

"Are you sure?" I asked.

"Yes. We can meet tomorrow and you can take me shopping at the specialty boutiques you told me about."

"Thank you, I appreciate your understanding. We rarely get the chance to see each other. Tell the driver you're going to the Dutch Inn. If I'm not at the club before one o'clock, ask Winston to drop you at the Park Plaza. It's on his way home. Maybe we can get a night cap back there."

"Perfect, it's a plan."

THE TIME WITH GLORIA went by too fast. We talked about her upcoming wedding, my healing and spiritual experiences in Egypt, my improved relationship with Robert, and even my comfortableness to leave the hot little gymnast with him.

Evil Ways

GINELLE SAT IN THE FRONT ROW, WATCHING THE BAND AND occasionally dancing with selected suitors. She had informed Robert of the change of plans. He couldn't help but notice her exceptionally proportionate figure, and her attractive legs showing beneath what could barely be called a dress. At the end of the night, she brought him a fresh cold ginger ale on the rocks and complimented him on the great music.

"Thank you. If you're ready, we can head out of here and I'll take you to the Plaza. Just give me a few minutes."

"Great, I'll grab my handbag and be right back."

Robert finished his drink, and with guitar in hand escorted Ginelle to his showstopper car. As they approached the car, he became fuzzy-headed and sleepy. Thinking it was fatigue, he opened the door for Ginelle and slid into the driver's seat. He realized something was amiss.

"What's the matter, Winston, something wrong? Not feeling yourself?" Ginelle asked. Before he could answer, she said, "Robert Sexton, my comrade. You look bad … really bad."

"You, you … bitch, you drugged me."

"That's right." Ginelle pulled out a forty-five and aimed it directly at his head. "Put these cuffs on and listen carefully, Mr. Sexton, this is what's going to happen. I gave you Burundanga. You'll have no resistance. The drug will make you compliant with everything I say. It'll last four hours, more than enough time to make the short drive to Winter Park. Now drive the speed limit and remember I have a very large gun."

Although under the influence, Robert's training, particularly with his trials of using various forms of pharmaceuticals, was about to kick in. He knew to slow his breathing and heart rate to lessen the effects of the drug commonly called Devil's Breath.

They arrived at the Park Plaza and there was no one around except a young desk clerk, who was more into reading his book than anything else. It was easy for Ginelle to hold onto Robert's arm as they passed through the lobby unnoticed, cuffs concealed by his jacket. Her gun, hidden in a large shoulder purse, remained pointed at him. As Ginelle guided the staggering Robert to her room, he pretended to be much more intoxicated than he was.

"So, the great Robert Sexton has finally met his match. You're worth one million American dollars, dead. How does it feel to be the one about to die, and at the hands of a woman?"

"So, I'm valued at a million," he mumbled. "A lot more than you'll ever be worth." If he made her angry, he knew the adrenalin rush would cause her to be unsteady, less accurate, and more likely to make a mistake.

Ginelle rubbed it in that she, a mere woman, had taken down the most dangerous and revered American spy. "Now I'm the one in control. How am I going to spend that money? Let me count the ways. Maybe I'll buy a car like yours. Maybe your precious Sally will need the money and sell me your car. Wouldn't that be ironic? Don't worry; I'll be there to comfort her as I did in Egypt. Then I'll kill her too."

"Possibly, but how are you going to prove you murdered me?"

"It's simple, *drägut*. I'm taking a picture of your dead body with today's newspaper and date."

Robert knew *drägut* meant sweetheart, and she was using it sarcastically. "Well, I have a better way."

"There's no better way. I'm going to kill you, take your picture, leave you here to rot in hell."

Cognizant of the gun, Robert kept her talking, looking for his moment. He asked, "Why do you kill for money? I never kill unless it's absolutely necessary. You lack honor, dignity. Merely Putin's puppet. Perhaps you're his *pizda tarfa*."

Calling her a cunt whore in her own language would more than likely put her over the edge. And it did. She lost her focus and reared up like a horse to strike him with the butt of her gun. As she did so, the barrel was no longer facing straight at him. Robert intercepted the blow and swung his cuffed hands hard enough to knock the gun to the floor. He wrapped his hands firmly around her neck.

In the ensuing fight, her gymnast body and skills served her well. She flipped up and over Robert and wrapped her muscular thighs around his neck. With his hands still cuffed, he did his best to punch into the meat of her thigh muscles to no avail. She was in great shape and mentally withstood the pain of the sharp, penetrating blow. Her thighs pressed on Robert's throat, blocking his airway. He had only twenty or thirty seconds of air left. He stood erect; her leg grip on his neck didn't loosen but now she was hanging slightly upside down in front of him. He ferociously swung her body into the bathroom doorway, slamming her into the jamb and breaking her back.

She died immediately.

ROBERT HEARD SOMONE KICK in the hotel room door, tearing it from the door jamb. Still standing over Ginelle's lifeless body, he was momentarily startled but ready for combat. He assumed it was her accomplice coming to finish the task.

As the door flew clear, Gloria and Rose rushed in.

Somewhat relieved, he said, "How did you guys find me?" Holding up his cuffed hands, he added, "I could use a little help here."

As Gloria uncuffed Robert, Rose explained. "David called me. Carakus had confirmed that Ginelle was KGB. He found evidence of an assassination plot. Ginelle was here to kill you!"

Ginelle's twisted body was still warm, eyes wide open, just a little blood seeping from the side of her head because her heart had stopped so suddenly when her back broke. She was wearing only one of her stilettos. Rose tried not to stare at the corpse and focused her attention instead on Robert.

"We got here as fast as we could. Gloria grabbed the young man at the desk and demanded Ginelle's room number. He only gave it to her after she put her .38 caliber revolver to his head. I'm so sorry. I delivered an assassin to you. I almost had you killed."

"I'm still standing, Rose! Stop the tears. No apologies. We were all fooled by an excellent warrior. You must always be mindful of Putin and his talents. He's skilled, and chose a woman assassin who almost succeeded. The moment she made a threat against you, she signed her own death certificate. She was going to play the same hand she played in Egypt, supportive friend until she determined how to murder you and leave the country without suspicion."

Still under the influence of the hypnotic drug, Robert added, "There was no way we were going to let that happen." He was referring to himself and his guardian angel.

"G, call the clean-up crew, and Rose, get Putin on the phone. It's 6:00 a.m. there. He should be starting his morning workout."

"I WARNED YOU, COMRADE, if you sent someone they'd die. Your Romanian agent is gone. Now I have you where I want you."

"How so, Sexton?"

"Remember the lessons of Khrushchev. He lost face to his American adversary, Kennedy. Although he did the righteous thing, he was dismissed as Premier and First Secretary of the Communist Party and forced to live a quiet life in exile. You came to your adversary and failed. You don't want your generals to know this. This botched attempt could be a crippling obstacle to your future. So, I tell you this now, stay away from me and my people or you will pay, conceivably the ultimate price."

"You try to threaten me, a soldier of the Soviet Union. I have no fear of you."

"Good words, but you do fear failure. If your name is ever associated with me in any form, I'll release to the Soviet press a full accounting of your failed effort on my life. Good day, comrade." Robert hung up.

"Hey, Rosie, remind me to send him an apple pie tomorrow."

Carry That Weight

I thought about was how much I had screwed up. I had almost gotten Robert killed. I should've known better in Egypt, been on alert when Ginelle pulled the Set card. My cards were dead on, and apparently so was hers. The standoff between Horus and Set. Thankfully, Horus the Hawk conquered, even with my epic mistake.

Timing had worked out where I could talk to Dr. Head in person without flying to Meade. He was giving an evening lecture at the Naval Air Warfare Center on the psychological effects of serving on a nuclear sub. He had some time to spare beforehand. Dr. Head was the father figure for several of us in the agency, but maybe even more for me. He always saw the good in people and taught us to accept ourselves as imperfect but wonderful human beings.

 Dr. Head said. "I assume this is one of Robert's specials."

I was driving a turquoise convertible Jaguar E-Type that Robert had bought me two weeks after the assassination attempt.

"Actually, this is mine, he bought it for me. He thought it would help me be in better spirits. It was Robert's over-the-top way of saying I should move on from the Ginelle episode."

I loaded Dr. Head's luggage into the trunk, and we drove to meet the Air Boss with the top down. The warm Florida breeze was a welcome sensation.

"Ooh la la, I just love looking at all these palm trees and orange groves. I see why you settled here. I suspected early on that you would tame and, what's that word when you put horses in a barn?—corral—that you'd corral Robert."

Dr. Head used the thirty-minute drive to counsel me and help me gain a new perspective on the situation. "You, my dear, have submerged into the darkness of guilt, like a submarine submerging into the darkness of the ocean. It's time to surface and see the light, like sailors who come to the surface to see the sunlight.

"Yesterday is gone, today is here, and tomorrow will take care of itself, if you let it. What happened is pretty simple. Ginelle was a top pro, hired by KGB to kill Robert. You're not a trained operative, you're a psychic. And there's something much deeper going on."

My spiritual awareness in Egypt, he explained, may have changed my life course. He suggested that I might be experiencing a crossroads in my young life, and he sensed that my days with the agency were drawing to an end. Since my return from Egypt, I had been pondering the idea of a life outside of the NSA. I felt guilty for wanting to leave, knowing I was in a relationship with a man who was devoted deeply to the agency. I also questioned if I was like my mother. Had I deliberately set out to put Robert in danger?

I shared a secret with Dr. Head. "My sister and I believe our mother has been poisoning our father, creating seizures enough to warrant an array of 911 emergencies. On my last visit, my father had told me he thought Mom was poisoning him. At first, I tried to rationalize that it was his dementia. I mean, who wants to believe their mother is capable of such an act? But I kept track of the calls, the hospital visits, and records, which showed he was immediately better once removed from his home environment."

"It's called Munchausen syndrome by proxy." Dr. Head said. "It's uncommon, but how is this relevant to you and Robert?"

"Maybe I still had trust issues with Robert, and I was subconsciously trying to harm the person closest to me. After all, I'm the one who showed a photo of him to Ginelle and delivered her straight to the million-dollar target."

He assured me that I wasn't like my mother, who clearly had a personality and mood disorder. He reminded me that I had undergone extensive psychological tests before receiving clearance for active duty.

"We had the indicators on your brother, Thomas. So trust me when I say that when you came on our radar, we learned everything about you, your family, and your lineage. You were there to write a political dossier. In my professional opinion, you're simply feeling guilty because it would've been devastating to lose Robert.

"Let me reiterate. Ginelle wasn't just any agent or novice; she was hand-picked to assassinate Robert. She posed as a tourist and used the lure of Egypt to distract your attention. She had a hundred times your experience in the business, and she knew to attack the weakest link in the chain. You weren't weak in your lack of loyalty but in your lack of experience."

Dr. Head shared that he had counseled other psychics and understood that when they're bombarded with many energies and stimuli, their psychic radar is affected.

"Let's recap the circumstances: you were in a foreign country, jet-lagged, lost luggage, on assignment, under the spell of Egyptian energies, and at the beginning of your own journey. And to add to that, you know what Robert's life involves and you can't allow your psyche to constantly be worried about him—he's always one step away from peril. Do you see what I'm trying to show you?"

"Yes, there was an overload of psychic influences."

"Remember this: TTT—Things Take Time."

We pulled into a parking space at the Navy base. A dozen or so sailors rushed over to see the Jag and politely asked if we needed help. Dr. Head thanked them but said we both had been here before. Nevertheless, the sailors escorted us to the main lecture room. All the time, they kept talking about my new car. I realized that Robert probably knew the car and I would attract attention. It was his way of helping me feel better about myself. The sailors were on the edge of flirting, but probably because of Dr. Head's presence, they acted like perfect gentlemen, as much as a group of young sailors could act as gentlemen.

We arrived at the cone-shaped hall which seated about six-hundred and was equipped with the latest technology, audio, and video. It was much like a small theater with excellent acoustics and high ceilings, pleasantly draped for sound. Commander Harris greeted us and Dr. Head introduced me. The commander said that he knew Robert and to send him his regards.

Dr. Head's audience was mostly sailors who had requested submarine duty. Our escort were among the seamen.

AFTER MY CONVERSATION with Dr. Head, I started to forgive myself for the incident. He had helped me understand that I'm not, nor shall ever be, a warrior, but rather a gentle spirit here to do wondrous things. Trying to use another Americanism, he said, "No harm, no foul; isn't that what Mr. Cosell always says?"

Dr. Head left me with these words, "Your journey has barely started."

Times They Are A-Changin'

WATCHING THE SUN GO DOWN, SIPPING FINE FRENCH WINE, AND enjoying the dogs by our side, Robert reached over in his chair and touched my leg. "Isn't our life wonderful, Rosie? We have a beautiful home and relationship. We eat and drink well and have a purpose."

I nodded in agreement, but thought to myself, *You've been shot, somebody tried to kill you, you've had to kill others. We're trying to live a normal life in between episodes of terror and mayhem. Is this what you want for us the rest of our lives?*

Robert must have been reading my mind. He said, "Remember asking me a while back about my goals and plans for our future?

"Yeah, you were working on something, but you weren't ready to share."

"Honey, I'm not psychic like you, but I had this epiphany, a more expanded version of my idea. I'm calling it, Homeland Shield of Security—HSOS. And I know how bureaucrats love acronyms."

"Bureaucrats, what are you thinking?"

Robert wanted to create a division that would focus on helping and protecting people in our own country. A concentrated department that would work with local, state, and federal authorities. The focus would be on finding missing children who end up in the sex trade at home and abroad, stopping priests from molesting children, removing drugs from our school, exposing corrupt judges. The aim wasn't to arrest and prosecute perpetrators. That required victims and lots of time, and we already had the FBI, state, and local police for that.

"I want to stop the criminals in their tracks."

"Isn't that like playing God? Being the judge, jury, and executioner, all without due process?"

"Where's due process for the twelve-year-old that's kidnapped, or the judge for the altar boy who is forced on his knees in the rectory at church? Most drug dealers are out on the street in twenty-four hours. The users get locked up."

"I believe in you. But not every agent is like a Robert Sexton."

"I don't have it all fleshed out. I made an appointment with Lang and Stevens; they may or may not go for it."

"Why Stevens? I've still never met the DCO."

"Most people haven't. He's a decent man, has dedicated his life to service. There's no point in talking to just Lang; he would need to run it up the flagpole. I need them both to salute the flag. They both know my reputation, have my personnel file, are well aware I've made sacrifices and that I had to kill or be killed because of political missions. They've been here a lot longer than me; they know what America is up against, both here and overseas."

Robert also knew what the agency was up against. We had a spy war inside our own American agencies. Currently, NSA was monitoring telephone calls and cable traffic of two prominent members of Congress who were making noise about our secret agency—Senator Frank Church, Democrat of Idaho, and Senator Howard Baker, Republican of Tennessee. Spying on our fellow Americans, definitely not the reason President Truman sanctioned—to protect the American people. We were now doing it for the self-preservation of the NSA.

It was interesting to learn what had been taking place within our government. For example, why J. Edgar Hoover, the director of the

FBI, was able to serve eight presidents and eighteen attorney generals. When a new president was inaugurated, the standard protocol was for the department heads, cabinet, and military secretaries to offer a letter of resignation. Most of the time they were replaced by the incoming president. Hoover, on the other hand, was never asked to resign when a new administration took over the White House. This was because he had spied on every new president and their executives and had dirt on all of them.

Even more fascinating, Robert's division had spied on Hoover and discovered his many tactics. Such as authorizing strong laxatives to be injected into the oranges consumed by political activists in order to cause havoc with their protests. He also approved of the FBI providing a diagram to the Chicago police that guided a shooter to kill the Black Panthers' leader, Fred Hampton. The FBI also had approval to keep tabs on nearly every notable writer in the country. And the list went on. The agency also knew Nixon frequently referred to Henry Kissinger as his "Jew Boy." That Betty Ford had been an alcoholic before and during her tenure as First Lady, and that …

I wanted to hear more, but Robert said, "Rosie, I have a special HSOS for you, aka Happy Sally Olivia Stone. I believe you'll find it in your healing and creativity."

"You're so clever. I could endorse that notion. Form an astral advisory board and enlist the assistance of angels, saints, spirit guides, enlightened loved ones, power animals, ascended healers."

"On that idea, this would be an excellent time to go in and design your studio."

"What studio?"

"The one I'm going to make for you in the loft."

ROBERT HAD NEVER USED that section of the house. The area was twenty by forty feet, with three bay windows, a Franklin stove in one corner, and a white high-gloss laminated ceiling that gave the room immense light and energy. He envisioned the healing table where I would have a beautiful view of the birds, a nice desk by the corner window where I could see the dogs running in and out of the woods, and my paints and canvasses at the far bay window. Given his ability to see space and know how to fill it, completion would be in a week or less.

He took my hand and led me to the stairs. "Now, let's go to the bedroom. I have new ideas for that space too. There's a gift waiting for you—aqua green lingerie from Hattie's, by your favorite French designer. I still don't understand why you love them—those expensive threads only stay on your bod mere seconds before I rip them off."

You Are So Beautiful

SINCE MY RETURN FROM EGYPT, I HAD FELT A HEIGHTENED DESIRE to create. Finally, with the help of everyone, I had managed to tap into all the beautiful memories of Egypt and leave behind the negative ones. One day I came into my studio, lit a candle and incense, and said a blessing for my healing space. Somewhere in that meditative state, I was transported back to the Nile, and I had a compulsive inspiration to paint. I infused the blank canvas with prayer and intuitively started spreading colors. I felt Sabria's spirit was guiding my hands throughout the process.

"HELLO ROSIE, WHERE ARE YOU? What room are you in?"

"I'm up here."

"Hey, babe, I see you've been painting by all the colors you're wearing. Now kiss me like you mean it."

"I might get paint on you." My clothes and exposed body parts were adorned with shades of burnt sienna, alizarin crimson, cadmium yellow, orange, and ivory black.

"I'll take my chances. Did you do this one while I was at HQ?"

"Yeah, I'm not sure if it's done." Robert was looking at a four by six canvas of an abstract version of three pyramids.

"Oh, it's done all right. I love it. What are you calling it?"

"The Call of Egypt."

"How about you come to the Call of Robert and give me a better kiss."

After I gave Robert a proper kiss, he sat down at my desk. As he watched me put away my paints and tools, I asked him to tell me how the Neptune Summit had gone.

THE GENERALS, ON THE WHOLE, were in favor of Robert's idea. They thought the plan would be challenging, but feasible. To work around the law would be complex. Their biggest concern was giving someone this much power. Aptitude, integrity, and stability were a must. They discussed a hierarchy, with Robert at the top of the chart. He'd be responsible for the three trial teams.

General Stevens had said funding and managing it secretly might prove to be too much, but to leave that to him. He had served America for forty-six years and run the agency for the last twelve, all under the radar of the congressional oversight committee. Skilled in navigating through the Suits, the general believed he could get that was needed. With Congress spending two trillion dollars a year, there had to be a way to find a million dollars for this experiment. Details would be fleshed out on their next meeting, after Robert had completed his assignment in Mexico.

"Rosie, it was kind of cool, but before I left, Stevens saluted me and said that he spoke for General Lang, President Carter, and our nation, and that they were all were indebted to me for my extraordinary service and sacrifice. The general smiled and said with a wink, 'Winston Forester, thank you for everything. Your uncle would've been proud of you.'"

"Aw, that had to make you feel good."

I had been so preoccupied after Egypt and the aftermath that I hadn't stayed abreast of what all was happening on Robert's front.

He was months into a drug sting, centered in Mexico City, involving the Colombians, Salvadorans, and Mexicans. Latinos were working together for the first time instead of fighting with each other. They had started a South American-style mafia cartel. It was in its infancy and these guys, "fuckers" Robert called them, wanted to make a name for themselves, much like Al Capone had done in Chicago in the twenties, to create an atmosphere of fear around them so people would leave them alone.

The operation sounded like something Robert would be eager to participate in. But he explained we were in it for the wrong reason. The agency was involved because of the money, not for the drugs. The various factions that produced coke and heroin had teamed up to form a cartel. They wanted to move American dollars, billions, out of our country and into the third-world drug lords' coffers. Russia held a strong influence in the region. They would love to control our back door as well as destabilize our economy with so much cash flowing out. As a bonus, they'd be destroying our schools and colleges by flooding them with massive amounts of drugs.

Robert stopped and looked at me. "It's why we call it a Cold War. They can land devastating blows to us without ever firing a weapon. And, baby, on another note, you'll need to pack your bags soon. We're both going to Mexico. You're going to be my cover as we go through customs. We're honeymooners spending time in the area. And you know what happens on honeymoons."

"Be serious."

"I am."

"Why do you need a honeymoon as a cover? You've been there before without me."

"Because I need to be there for at least a week or more to set up the sting we're planning."

Robert's job was to figure out the players. He was working with a small gang of six: two Mexican brothers, the Zapatas, and the rest were all foreigners: Escobar, Fuentes, Ramirez, and one other.

"They're despicable, mean, nasty individuals. Worse than the mafia."

"How so?"

"They have no legitimate morals at all. The mob doesn't mess with family or kill police. They have some respect for life; they kill only for business. These fuckers kill for sport. You won't be near them. They already know me as the mule moving the merch for them. I'm operating under the premise that my money people want to see the quality of the coke and also be sure they can supply large amounts on demand."

The setup was to move five to ten kilos a month, roughly a million per trip, with a kilo averaging around 150,000 dollars. "It's all about greed. You hook them with large numbers because that's what motivates them."

Robert had made two trips with small amounts to test the waters and thought he had gained their confidence. They knew Robert to be a slick operator. He'd never show up with a million-and-a-half dollars, there would be no incentive to go through with the trade. They'd kill him and keep the money and the drugs and find a new mule if he was that stupid.

The goal was to capture them but not kill them, break them down for contacts, where they get their supply, where the labs were, who was bankrolling the manufacturing. He would stage a house for them to collect their money, a place where they would feel safe. Six armed men versus him with no weapons. If the strategy worked, they would be unprepared for what awaited them.

"What awaits them?"

"As soon as they enter the house, about twenty armed undercover agents. Enough firepower they'll either surrender or die. No time to raise their weapons. But if you remember, I was on the other side of something like that."

"Bogota, how could I forget?" *And,* I thought, *what if this plan fails?*

"IT'S ALL GOING DOWN on Saturday, the tenth. We'll have a week before to enjoy our honeymoon. While I'm doing the deal, you'll be at the hotel, out of harm's way. You can be by the pool, drinking your margaritas and tanning that sexy body of yours. Let's forget about all that for right now. Let's walk down to the brook."

We hiked a mile along a passage that Robert had cleared with a hand sickle through the heavily wooded area. Robert wanted the dogs to stay at the house. When we arrived, the stream was crystal clear. Robert stopped and turned to me. He held out his hands, and I placed mine on top of his, just like the first time I met him at Dr. Head's office. He looked deeply into my eyes and said, "I have something for you." Robert reached into his pocket and pulled out a beautiful diamond ring. It had two round stones set in an infinity symbol, with smaller ones along with the band. He placed it on my ring finger.

"My angel girl, you know I love you; will you marry me?"

I was stunned. My mind raced back to the first time I had laid eyes on him. I was in a Neptunian dream, then and now.

"On this planet," said Robert, "we use words."

Although I was speechless, in another state, one of ecstasy, I wrapped my arms around him and said, "Yes, I will!" I had doubted that he would ever be ready for marriage. I had suspected that he might always be the Hawk on the hunt for a variety of prey. When I came back to earth, Robert was talking.

"I figured, why play at it? Let's get engaged and enjoy a pre-honeymoon."

"Are we really engaged? The ring fits perfectly on my hand. Is this ring real or is this part of the cover?"

"Yes, it's real. I'll put you in charge of when and where we tie the knot. There's plenty of time to plan our future. You can do your astrological voodoo and see when the stars are shining on us to take the leap."

In the stream was an ice bucket with a bottle of Ruinart champagne. He pulled two glasses from the bucket and filled them. "Simply, to us," he whispered as the glasses clinked. After several sips, he set our glasses down on a smooth round stone and began undressing me. Within seconds we were both naked, and he picked me up and gently laid me down in a shallow part of the stream. We made love for an hour as the water trickled around our bodies and as we finished our bottle of bubbles.

PLAYING THE ROLE OF newlyweds came effortlessly, and we sold it well. We made it through customs with no problem. We managed lots of hugging and kissing as we arrived in the little township of LaCondesa, an upper-class suburb of Mexico City, where many Europeans lived. Our hotel was close to the cartel's safe house, where Robert had been on his previous visits.

The week went by all too quickly. We made love until dawn, took long walks in the park, had romantic dinners. One evening, Robert picked up a guitar from a strolling minstrel and sang "You're So Beautiful" to me. It was like a dream.

Unfortunately, the dream ended, and Saturday arrived. I woke up with what I imagined morning sickness must feel like. I did the math: I was late on my period.

Live and Let Die

ROBERT SAID GOODBYE MID-MORNING AND THAT HE WOULD CALL around four o'clock when the deal was done. ADCO Lang had given him two team leaders for support on the ground. If something changed with the arrangement, Dick Nichols or Hunter Redmond would contact me.

There were no margaritas by the pool. I crawled back into bed, nauseated, and fell asleep. When I woke up from a jarring and chaotic dream, it was well past four o'clock. As I paced the floor, my hands grew warm. I felt energy radiating from them, intense and uncomfortable. I flashed back to Egypt and tried to turn my thoughts on Robert when the phone rang.

"Rose, it's Dick Nichols. Sexton hasn't checked in. Have you heard from him?"

"No, I haven't. I was hoping you were him."

"Redmond and I will be outside your door shortly. We're picking you up and going to the area of Robert's last known whereabouts. We'll discuss details on the way."

AS WE ARRIVED AT the cartel safehouse, a police car pulled up. The officer, one of our connections with the Mexico City police, Sergeant Alverez, read us the handwritten account that had just come in from an eyewitness.

Mannford Dunkel recounted: *A bunch of Latinos and one American broke into my house. They hit me with a baseball bat, I fell to the ground. They grabbed my wife and threw my two kids in the closet. One of them threw a suitcase on the table, opened it and took out a gun. He gave the gun to the American and told him to put it in my mouth. They took my wife to the bedroom.*

I was left in the room with the American. He whispered forcefully in my ear, 'Don't talk, listen. We only have seconds. I'm sorry I can't stop the first one from attacking your wife. The gun I'm holding isn't loaded.' He handed me a knife that had been taped to his calf. He said, 'This is what you have to do: soon as we hear the first scream from your wife, yell as loud as you can "DEA stole your drugs." I'll grab the suitcase with the drugs and run out the door. They'll chase me, except the son of a bitch fucking your wife. As soon as the others run out after me, go in and stab him as many times as you can in the middle of the back and stick the knife in his neck.'

Then he grabbed me by the back of my neck, pulled our foreheads together, and said, 'You got a job to do. If you don't kill him, he'll kill your wife, you, and your kids.' His plan worked. I heard my wife scream, he ran, I yelled. Just as he said they would, they all chased after him except the one on top of my wife. I did what he said, stabbed the guy in the back a dozen times and the throat. Called the police. That American saved me, my wife, my kids.

Chills went up and down my spine in the limited time I had to comprehend the magnitude of the story. I told the sergeant, "There's no way they could've caught up with Robert. He can outrun anybody, even carrying ten pounds of cocaine."

Nichols added, "Unless he wanted to be caught."

Redmond agreed and said, "Let's spread out and search the area on foot. We each have a whistle: blow it as loud as you can if you find anything. Rose, if you get anything psychically, let us know."

Three blocks away, I turned intuitively into what appeared to be a small road, but instead it was a dingy alley. At first glance it seemed deserted, just debris from a dozen trash cans and a dumpster far off in the rear. The buildings that formed the alley were rundown with broken windows and paint peeling everywhere. There were no streetlights, just a couple of back doors for the businesses in front. As I entered the alley, about two hundred feet away, I spotted what looked like a jackal-dog hybrid with pointed ears, sitting quietly. As I drew closer, I saw he was guarding a lifeless body. I could feel the dog's thoughts. The Egyptian deity, Anubis, ran through my mind. *Oh my God, it's Robert! Blood everywhere!*

I blew my whistle as loud as possible. As I hovered over him, Robert was fading fast. I shouted, "Stay alive, Robert. Breathe, open your eyes. Don't give up. Keep breathing. Move your body. Breathe."

My hands spontaneously rose over Robert's torso, palms face down, almost as if they scanned his body like an x-ray machine. Heat transmitted in both directions, leaving my hands and rebounding off his body. I felt compelled to keep doing this, unsure what was truly happening. Enormous energy, much like an electrical current, ran through my body. It seemed as though fog or mist enveloped our space.

Nichols and Redmond arrived together and ran over. But before they had the chance to touch him, I shouted, "Stand back!"

"He's bleeding, Rose," said Nichols.

"I know, trust me."

"I hope you know what you're doing," said Redmond. "He's losing blood fast. He's dying."

Something greater than me guided me. I believe I was God's instrument, being led by a higher force both physically and mentally. Before I could respond to Redmond, he said, "Oh my God, the bleeding has slowed down right in front of our eyes."

A minute later, Robert's bloody hazel eyes opened. I gained control over my hands and caressed his head. Burning heat still emanated from my hands. What we observed next was nothing short of a miracle. A forceful Being reached beneath his nearly lifeless body and in an instant jolted him to a sitting position. Even a healthy Robert couldn't move that fast. We all witnessed the phenomenon. We saw a heavenly glow while experiencing an intense sensation of bewilderment. It had to be a Divine intervention. Without anyone noticing, the dog had disappeared. Next to Robert's body was a thick, long, white feather.

Robert was taken to the hospital. Most of the bleeding had stopped before we arrived. There he received plenty of morphine. Abundant prayers were offered by the whole team, whether spoken or not. We were all in the room when he awakened.

"Where am I?" We barely heard his whisper due to the damage his trachea and vocal cords had sustained.

"Honey, you're in the hospital."

"Did the family make it?"

"Yes, all of them," replied Redmond.

"Did we get them?"

"No," said Nichols.

His eyes closed. I pulled up his covers and quietly said, "I love you, Robert. We were all afraid of losing you."

I asked the guys to let him go back to sleep and assured them that I'd stay with him until transport arrived. The ADCO had medical transport already on the way. It was a short stay at the hospital, and then we were flown to Walter Reed.

GENERAL LANG AND DAVID both understood that there would be no debriefing for at least a week because of Robert's condition. I didn't leave his side. Several days later, with a stronger voice, he began to tell me the missing parts of the story that only he had lived.

"We were on the way, drugs in hand, to our safe house where the money was stashed. At the last minute, they threw in a test to see if I was one of them. We broke into an apartment to rape and kill a family.

"They locked the kids in the closet. They all took the woman into the bedroom except Escobar, who handed me a gun he took from the drug suitcase. Of course, I knew he would never give me a loaded gun. He said, 'Put it in the German's mouth. Don't kill him; let him hear his wife being raped by each of us.'

"I knew when they were done with the wife, they'd probably rape the husband, slit his throat, then kill the children in front of her, and make me the one to do it."

"Oh my gosh."

"Yeah, these guys are insanely sick fuckers. They get an enormous rush of adrenalin from raping and killing. Escobar went into the bedroom. He turned before walking out and said, 'Don't worry, gringo, you'll get a turn.' I had seconds to make a plan. I knew the way to save the family was to make myself the target. There is one thing they love more than terrorizing, and that's money. Taking the drugs is taking their money. I quickly told the German what he had to do, then I grabbed the case with the drugs and ran out of the apartment. I knew they would follow me."

"What happened? I mean, your speed?"

"When I ran, I kept them close enough so they'd think they might catch me. If I disappeared, some or all would go back and kill the family. The flaw in my plan was that I didn't know the terrain and ran into a dead-end alley.

"The five caught up to me. Escobar put the tip of his gun to my forehead and cocked the hammer. In the heat of the moment, he was about to pull the trigger. I had to get him not to shoot me. A gunshot would be quick and painless but allow no chance of survival for the family: there would be time for these guys to return and continue doing harm. If I kept them engaged long enough the cops would show up, and they'd run."

"What did you say?"

"I didn't say anything, it's what I did. Made the sign of the cross as if I was doing my last rites. I knew Escobar wouldn't shoot while I made the gesture. They were all Catholics and wearing crosses."

Robert paused and cleared his throat. "I need a sip of water."

"So, you're alive because you drew the cross! You played on their religion."

"Yes, how fucked up is that? Kind of like the mob. They go to church on Sunday, nobody dies. And the other days of the week if they walked by a church, they stop and make the sign of the cross, and then go kill.

"Well, Escobar had a moment to think, and said, 'Killing is too good for you.' The sadistic bastard wanted to take pleasure terrorizing and inflicting pain. So instead of shooting me, he started beating me, and the other four joined in."

"Oh, Robert … you don't have to finish. I read the German's account, and I can physically see you, and I read the doctor's report. It's a bit overwhelming."

"No, I need to tell you. At least this one time. It helps me to get clarity before I debrief."

"Okay, I'm listening. I'm here for you."

"I fell to the ground and they kicked me for maybe three minutes. Three minutes doesn't sound long, but it's all day when you're being stomped, punched, and hit. With each blow my entire body and mind absorbed the shock. These guys hit with full force each time. Blow by blow, my body was exposed to their evil energy.

"One had a bat and broke my ribs. He tried to break my knee but missed and broke my leg. The bone tore through my pants. I couldn't see, hear, or think of anything. About fifty or so blows into the assault, I began to feel nothing. In my mind, however, I relived my life. I saw myself at two years old, ten years old, graduating from high school, and our home together. Suddenly my mind shifted to: How did I get here? Why was I here? How am I going to escape this? A few minutes later I heard police sirens. The onslaught continued briefly. By this time I was completely defenseless. It ended after each took a turn squarely kicking me in the balls. You don't understand how much pain there is being kicked in the balls, you don't have them, but it's excruciating."

"No, I can't imagine."

"I thought they had beaten me to death. My eyes were heavy and bloody. Blood seeped from every opening in my body. I felt death nearing. I lay motionless for what seemed like an hour, but I don't really know how long it was. I was ready to die, felt life draining out of me. Then something jerked me fiercely and lifted me. I opened my eyes and there you were."

I WAS MORE IN LOVE with Robert than ever before and had more admiration and respect for him than one can imagine. He had risked his life and endured a horrendous beating to save a family of four. It was the most selfless thing anyone could do, to be willing to die for people he didn't even know. Robert could've run away and been safe; instead, he had made himself the target.

It was easy for me to apply Robert's love of baseball, and the analogy of playing ball, to what he had done. When Robert took that suitcase full of coke and ran, for that one moment in time, he was the best centerfielder that played for the best team. It was like the last game of the World Series, the bottom of the ninth, bases loaded with two strikes, two outs and a blazing fastball speeding toward him. As providence would have it, he swung and hit it deep. Instead of rounding the bases to tens of thousands of cheers, he was alone. Incredibly alone. That's what warriors do.

It dawned on me that most people are never tested like that. They go through life not knowing how they would react in a life-and-death moment. He had sacrificed his life, his health, his future. And only a handful of people, his angels, and God would ever be aware of his heroic act.

I wondered how he was going to cope. I wondered how I was going to cope. I wanted out of the NSA, and I wanted Robert out too.

Time Has Come Today

ONE MONTH AFTER MEXICO, GENERAL STEVENS CALLED FOR AN emergency meeting with his core team leaders and important personnel. Robert, still in recovery mode, remained at home. General Lang had insisted I attend in Robert's stead. As uncomfortable as I was being there instead of Robert, it was more unnerving to leave him alone for a whole day.

I arrived at the base at 0800, signed in, and headed to Neptune to join David, Gloria, and Dr. Head. This arrival was more than marginally different from any other. I could not stop my mind from evaluating how much irrevocable damage our lives had endured. Our association with the NSA had taken a huge toll on us. I didn't really know if Robert would recover. I was thankful he had made it out of Mexico, but what about the next assignment or the one after that? Would it ever end?

Everyone was excited to see me, and all asked how Robert was doing. Still, my presence and Robert's absence seemed all wrong.

We went into the assembly room—a medium-sized, brightly lit chamber, sterile and soundproof. It had a sizable table that could seat more than twenty people and was equipped with the best technology—large flat screens that only the military possessed. Robert referred to this room, where most of the strategic planning took place, as the Strat box, also called the War Room II. When General Stevens walked in, we stood at attention until he said, "At ease and have a seat." He was a pleasant-looking man, early to mid-sixties. He wore his uniform well, adorned with many medals from WWII, Korea, and Vietnam. When he took off his cap, he began to speak. "We're going to have a conversation that is off the record. This meeting will have never happened. And each of you is to take Neptune to the grave. It does not nor ever has existed."

He got right to the point. Congress, Senator Church in particular, had been running an investigation into our activities. Church had gone on *Meet the Press* a couple of years before and alluded to an organization that seemed to be describing the NSA. But with no facts, he could not name the National Security Agency as the target of his investigation. The general accounting office decided to do their probe and the Oversight Committee came in. Billions of dollars had to be accounted for by the DOD. It was easy to float money with war, but Vietnam was over.

General Stevens said that within seventy-two hours a story would be published in the Washington Post, "The Unmasking of America's Secret Agency." As soon as the congressional dossier came across the president's desk, the chief of staff, Hamilton Jordan, had arranged a conference with only General Stevens and President Carter in the Oval Office.

After thirty minutes of intense discussion, the general and the president had come up with a plan. They decided to cooperate fully with the media and acknowledge the existence of the NSA since its inception in 1952. However, they would reveal only the fifteen thousand employees who worked above the surface. They would disclose the NSA as a surveillance agency that spies on America's enemies. There would be no acknowledgment about the depth of surveillance perpetrated on other federal agencies or the American public. Covert Operations would remain a secret.

The division would continue to work for two more years on the funding that was already in place. It couldn't exactly return millions of dollars to the DOD without creating a massive red flag. This way, the dark operatives could complete all projects and missions currently in play. The few remaining agents could transition to the CIA. Only nine remained out of fifty; Robert was one of them. Most of them had died on overseas missions.

The Spooks department would go public as if it were a new division. Offices would move to above ground within three days. We were never to disclose that we were part of the covert operations. Instead, we were to admit that the NSA was experimenting with paranormal research to help in the country's defense, but never divulge that any of our methods worked or had ever been used in the field.

Going forward, our salary and expenses would have to be justified. Instead of being paid in cash, we would be treated like the rest of the DOD. This would require budget approval from the House Armed Services Committee. For the first time, we would have a paper trail. David more than likely would be under heavy scrutiny and forced to take measures to strengthen our department and show Congress the cost-effectiveness of the agency. This meant that Congress was coming for a visit.

The president would be signing into law the Foreign Surveillance Information Act on the 25th of October, 1978, exactly twenty-six years and one day after the NSA was created. This FISA was the culmination of Senator Church's years of investigation. A compromise had been worked out to leave Truman's memo as the basis for the NSA's existence. No statute, act, or any other document would be ratified.

Near the end of the meeting, General Stevens announced that we would have a close friend in Congress, as Anthony Grogan was expected to win his congressional bid to represent New York's 11th district. Before dismissing everyone, the general asked to speak with me, David, and Roger privately in his office. The sound of his voice saying my name gave me an uneasy feeling, although I didn't know why. Perhaps it was because he had always been the unknown factor that controlled everything we did at Neptune.

In his office, he asked, "How is our warrior doing?" I told him that Robert was struggling but was determined to make a full recovery. After a brief discussion, he gave me his card with his personal number and said, "Call me if you or Robert need anything. I mean anything. All our resources are available for you."

"Yes sir, thank you."

He saluted me and said, "No ma'am, thank you."

He sure knew how to make an exit.

I'm Still Standing

ROBERT WENT OUT FOR AN EARLY MORNING WALK. HE INSISTED ON doing it alone. Vivid images of his struggle to move his broken body were still fresh in my mind. For the last two months I had taken care of him, barely leaving his side since the day we returned from Mexico. I had to lock the dogs outside of the bedroom at night so they wouldn't jump in bed and hurt him. Little did I know when Robert built my studio that I'd be using it to rebuild what was once a magnificent warrior. Every morning for two months I had laid my hands on him and asked for a Divine healing.

In addition to my efforts, I had abided by the doctor's conventional orders. I had moved Robert as much as he could tolerate, lifted each arm off the bed one at a time, bent his knees, tried to make his legs and feet rise ever so slightly off the mattress, fed him protein shakes through a straw, held up an eye chart and made him read as much as possible, then rest and do it again several times each day.

But an hour had passed and he hadn't returned from his walk. As I dressed to go find him, I heard the door. I ran through the house to find him.

"Slow down, babe."

"God, I love you. You haven't called me babe in months."

"Rosie, that can't be true."

"It is. You also haven't called me Rosie either, or even smiled."

"I'm okay. I didn't break any speed records, but I made it around the hiking path, one point four miles. I'm not ready for work yet, but I'm back."

"Are you freaking serious? You can't ever go back to work. I almost lost you in Mexico. I am not taking that risk again. Are you going to stay at this until your luck runs out? I forbid it. You can't …"

"Hold on. Slow it down. Take a breath. Listen to me. We already talked about a major change in the way I do business. Remember HSOS?"

I was too furious to pay attention. I knew his work was important. But how many more people did he have to save? Who would be there when he needed saving? Only months ago, Robert had questioned if we were making a difference or had become unwitting pawns in this Cold War, supporting violence in the name of politics. The agency had undergone so many changes since Robert had become part of the experiment his uncle set in motion in 1965. Today's missions were propaganda-driven, communism versus democracy, and that might never end.

Robert reminded me that in the future he would be more like a cop than a spy. I was still uncomfortable with the work and his chances of survival. Instead of arguing, he lifted me and held me in his arms. His strength had returned, and it was like someone had attached a wire and run a thousand volts of electricity through him. His eyes were wide, clear, and dancing, like they used to be. Even his hair looked different. He explained that he had evoked the power of my sessions, the energy from my hands, and recreated our daily time together in his mind as he had walked. His stride had lengthened and his legs had moved a bit faster. Before too long, he had begun feeling much better.

"You've healed me, Rosie. Now my job is to get my body back in shape. Tomorrow I'm going to the track." He kissed me on the cheek, put me down, slapped me lightly on the butt and said, "Can you find my Yankees shirt?"

"It's great that you want to wear your shirt again. You realize you can't run quite yet. You're hardly walking."

"True, but it's time to move into the next phase of my recovery. I miss being me, that confidence of knowing that wherever I am, that I'm in control, with no fear."

"To me, you've always been you. Just because you were injured doesn't mean you were less of a man. My admiration for you has doubled since Mexico. No one else would have sacrificed what you did and endured the damage you went through. You're amazing."

"I'm scheduled to meet with the urologist this week. I'll find out more about the aborted testicle and how that'll affect my ability to perform."

"I'm in for the long haul. Of course, I love our sex life, but there's nothing more important than you. Besides, you'll always be great in that department."

"How can you be sure?"

"I'm psychic, and I'm a woman."

I briefly talked with Robert about my insecurities with my healing abilities. He was the biggest believer in my healing power and strength, yet something was missing. I still didn't understand the Living Sea Scrolls. They were a colossal mystery, and I had no idea what to do with them. Every time I started to open and read them, I feared that the parchment would fall apart. They seemed so fragile, more like the Dead Sea Scrolls.

Robert reached over and held my hand. "Apparently it's not your time to understand the meaning. Didn't you tell me that Sabria said the scrolls would find you when the time and place is right? Perhaps the ARC healing is meant for someone other than me. Regardless of the scrolls, I know something you're doing is working. I look forward to our healing every day. Each session is different." He talked about the variations.

In the beginning, he had slept through most of the sessions. When awake, he felt he was in a dream-like state. My hands were sometimes so hot he thought they were going to burn him. He experienced tingling sensations throughout his body, particularly his extremities. Often, he sensed the presence of something larger and unworldly was in the room with us.

"You're a gifted healer, and I'm a walking testament to your powers. I know you say you're just the vessel, but to me, you're much more. It's easy to see the physical changes, but the emotional changes are profound, too."

Robert reminded me of his recurring nightmare of the eleven children from Hungary, where their parents closed in on him, asking why he let them die. That dream had changed directly after a session when he had fallen asleep on my healing table. The sequence had started as usual, but then a sense of warmth overtook the mood of the dream. A woman's voice had spoken on his behalf to the throng of protesters. The atmosphere had gone from guilt and anxiety to peaceful resolution.

The woman asked in a gentle soft voice for the children to follow her, which they eagerly did. She gracefully turned towards the parents and told them not to be adversarial and accusatory towards him and that he had hardly been more than a child himself when this tragic event took place. It was time for all to move on. Robert described her voice as surreal, not of this earth, with a soothing, angelic quality that made his vision feel unquestionably genuine.

I had been reading and learning about healing and discovered it's common for old emotional scars to resolve during a session. When I was working on the physical, the angels were working something deeper—emotionally, mentally, and spiritually.

"Rosie, the difficult question for me is, are guardian angels with you all the time or only on an as-needed basis? Sometimes they don't guard, they rescue. Other times they guide. Are the same guardian angels assigned to you all the time, or are there different ones with different responsibilities?"

I told Robert that I had been working on a book, *Spark-el,* that addressed some of his questions. It was an inspirational tale that explored the pilgrimage of the soul on an inner journey to the heart. "Seven different kinds of angel sparks are discovered along the way. Embodied in the story are the symbolic language and teachings that have endured through time, the Bible, the Kabbala, esoteric astrology, Hindu philosophy …"

"Why haven't I read it?"

"It's not finished yet. Now that your eyes are working well again, I'll find the draft and let you read it."

I could tell he was growing tired. He had had enough progress for the day. I wanted to tell him about the changes at the agency, with Neptune.

Egypt had changed me—my perspective, my energy, my desires. Mexico had changed me too. I was quite clear in that I never wanted to go through anything like Robert's beating again. I came so close to losing him, all in the name of senseless violence. But for now, it was good enough to know he was healing. We could talk about the NSA another time.

I Can See Clearly Now

FOUR MONTHS AFTER MEXICO, ROBERT HEADED BACK TO MEADE. The base was the same; there was no problem getting through gate security, but some things at the NSA building had changed. Rose and the Spooks no longer reported to Neptune. When Robert entered the reception area, Meredith, the long-time receptionist, was absent. He was greeted by an unfamiliar face.

"Who are you, and do you have an appointment?"

"I'm Robert, here to see the ADCO."

"We don't have an ADCO here. And, Robert who?

"Sexton, I'm here to see General Lang."

"I'm sorry, but you're not on the books."

"You must need a scorecard. I don't need an appointment." Robert turned away from the receptionist and went toward the elevators.

"Where are you going."

"To see Roger Lang."

"Stop, or I'll call security."

"Honey, I am security. You do what you want, but I'm going to his office. Why don't you call the general?"

"Well, I might."

The secretary made a call. "Sir, a Robert Sexton is here, wait, where did he go?"

"Let it go, Barbara. Look at the monitor; he's already in the elevator. Why don't you ask around the pool? Find out for yourself who you tried to stop. You must remember, before they can reach you, they've been cleared at the gate. Your job is to announce arrivals and take signatures, not to interrogate. It's best you remember that you're new. Try to fit in."

While everything looked the same, Robert sensed things were very different. When he got off the elevator, there were still uniformed Marines brandishing M16 rifles and SIG hand-guns, but all were new faces. Yet these new soldiers knew who Robert was. They asked for the mandatory ID, saluted him, and allowed him to go ahead.

"ROBERT, FORGIVE THE GIRL in the reception. Her daddy is a congressman. I was coerced into hiring her. Unfortunately, she's one of many changes now that we're under the examination of Congress, particularly the Oversight Committee. I had to send part of our usual Marine detail topside with the Spooks. These leathernecks are very well trained. I'm sure Rose filled you in on the meeting that never was."

Robert shook his head. "Yes."

"How the hell are you back so fast? I thought you'd be out at least six to eight months. The last time I saw you, you couldn't move on your own. You could barely talk."

Robert attributed his recovery to Rose's healing and energy powers. After one week, his injuries began to recover at an accelerated rate. Bruises and lacerations went away in a matter of days. Bones knitted back together in weeks, not months. He gave credit to the doctors and dentists who also contributed to his mending, but he recognized that without Rose he could have spent a year in the restoration process.

"I'm back and ready for an assignment, sir."

"Okay, just don't pick me up." The general remembered when he had prematurely written Robert off. "No need to prove you're okay, I can see that. Has Rose talked to David about her healing activities?"

Robert informed General Lang that Rose was retiring from active duty to pursue and expand her abilities. She would be transitioning soon to private practice but had agreed to be available as an outside resource for any national emergency.

The general sighed. "I always felt that she was on loan. The Tuck incident still sends chills up my spine, and I'm a battle-scarred general with three active war tours. We were blessed to have her as long as we did."

"She's also been painting lately and is sending you a piece designed especially for your office. It's her way of thanking you for all you've done for both of us. And her way to brighten up your walls."

"I look forward to it. You know how much we'll miss her, but of course, I wish her the best. Now, would you like to hear the HSOS program details?"

"Yes, sir, that's why I'm here."

"General Stevens got the president to commit to funding our existing projects and four future ones. HSOS is one of them. So now that the capital is in place, we're ready when you're ready."

General Lang explained to Robert that regardless of their respect for him, this experiment would call for constant supervision. Even though secrecy was in their DNA, there could be no secrets between them. Throughout America's history, there had always been unseen, unsung heroes skirting the laws to keep the people safe. "If it is necessary, it is legal." However, to give an agent this kind of autonomy could be dangerous for Robert, the generals, and the DOD.

The experimentation would be in three cities with Robert responsible for the actions of all three teams. Robert would be stationed in Lexington, Kentucky. Exemplary agents Hunter Redmond and Dick Nichols would be placed in Evansville and Cincinnati, respectively. Both agents would report directly to Robert on a daily basis. All three would pose as US Marshalls and have support from FBI, state police, and local law enforcement. No one would know of their NSA connection. The general concluded that everything must be sanctioned by him ahead of execution.

"Robert Sexton will be quietly buried by the end of the year. When you make a final decision on when you want to move, your FBI contact and coordinator will be Terrence Crowley."

Terry was a thirty-year FBI veteran, fifty-nine years old, also the Special Agent in charge of the Indianapolis office. He had served eight years as an MP in the Marines before going to college, and then earned a law degree. Tuck and Terry had served in the Corps together.

"When you're ready, I'll call Terry and fill him in, on a need-to-know basis, of course. We'll convene at a later date with General Stevens and have a much more detailed meeting. Keep me abreast of your timeline."

"Yes, sir. I will."

"And send Rose my best. Tell her I said she should be proud of her service to our country." The general paused, "Never mind, I'll send her a letter myself."

Homeward Bound

BY THE SPRING OF 1980 WE HAD MARRIED AND WERE LIVING IN Hopewell, Kentucky, in the house we had spotted a few years earlier. Our Winter Park home was exceptional, but somehow Winston managed to make our new home even better. He began working on the forty-year-old house as soon as we arrived. Winston loved architecture and building; it was one of the ways he coped with the arduous demands of his cloak-and-dagger lifestyle.

He started by remodeling the bathroom in the master bedroom. Knowing my love for taking baths, he installed an oversized copper bathtub as well as quartz countertops with copper fixtures. He knocked out a wall and created a spacious dressing room for my abundant clothes, shoes, and accessories. The upstairs had four small bedrooms that he made into two rooms, a spiritual healing room and an art studio.

The home and town seemed like the perfect place to write and create. The dogs adjusted well enough to the move, pretty much happy they were with us. They still had a large yard in which to run and a new home to explore and learn. We did miss the bird aviary, especially Winston. His morning ritual had been meditating among the winged creatures. Fortunately, we found the perfect buyer for our Florida home, a life-long ornithologist. We knew the aviary was in good hands.

Our decision to move to Hopewell coincided with Winston's transition into his new line of work. His office in Lexington was only a forty-five-minute drive. I had great comfort in knowing that Putin, or any other adversary, would not put this small, quaint city on their radar.

Another influence for moving back to my home state was that Winston believed, deep down, I wanted to return to my roots. As he would say, "You can take the girl out of Kentucky, but you can't take Kentucky out of the girl." There was some truth to that. I did desire to resolve and heal my relationship with the Crazy Stones, particularly my mother, if there was any possible chance. We would have to wait and see if being in a nearby city, rather than states away, would turn out to be a bonus or a drawback.

Winston and I still had trouble with our names. It seemed that Robert was his real name, and Winston more like his cover. I met him as Robert, but I thought Winston was fitting for him. It was English, derived from Wynn and Stan, meaning joyful stone. He sure had made me a joyful Sally Stone. Winston often called me Sally Rose, and that worked too.

EARLY ONE MORNING, my mother phoned. It was about my father. According to her, his dementia had progressed to Alzheimer's. My first thought that my mother was just up to her old tricks, making him out worse than he was. But I didn't really think that was the case this time, because years ago his attacks had miraculously ended after I confronted my mother with my suspicion regarding his seizures and told her that I would notify the doctors and involve the police if necessary. Nevertheless, my mother was working hard to have my father moved out of the house and into a nursing home. She said a room had finally become available at the Thomson-Hood Veterans Center in Wilmore.

I decided to see my father before he was transported to the center. I was much better prepared to handle my mother than before. There was now a name for my mother's behavior. It was called Borderline Personality Disorder. I had read about the signs and symptoms listed in the *Manual of Mental Disorders* that Dr. Head had sent to me. After reading about it, I concluded that my mom was a textbook case. Intense fear of abandonment, check. Rapid shifts in mood, check. Anger and rage, check. Impulsive behaviors, check. Vindictive to family members, check. It would be a close tie between my mother and Joan Crawford in *Mommie Dearest.*

On my visit, my mother was on exceptionally good behavior due to the company in the house. My father's longtime friend, Colonel Haile, better known as Kern, was visiting him also. They had served together in World War II as military police.

The colonel and I started talking, and he asked me if I'd be interested in substitute teaching for him at the Millersburg Military Institute. He was taking a small leave of absence to do research, and the principal was having a hard time finding a substitute. My mother had told him I wasn't working. In her mind, I never had a real job.

The invitation to teach at a military school, while interesting, didn't seem to fit with my greater desire to paint or heal. Even though I was still looking for a place outside the home to do my readings and healing, I had not found the right space. I reserved working at home for clients I knew; with Winston's past and present, we did not want strangers in our house. When Winston arrived home, I got his opinion.

"What would you be teaching if you took the job?" he asked.

"World History."

"Well, wouldn't that be fortuitous as a former NSA agent from the Cold War. What did you tell the colonel?"

"I told him that I would talk to my husband and get back with him in a couple of days."

"I think you'd make a great teacher, but you're already pretty busy. If you take the teaching job, are you going to show 'em your gun, Casallie?"

"Of course not, I turned it in. Perhaps I should have kept it. I do remember what a ladies man you were, and if you were ever to go down that road again, I might just need it."

"You better be kidding."

"I am."

"By the way, I'll be gone tomorrow for the day. Meeting Terry Crowley in Lexington."

"Your FBI guy in the region?"

"Yes. We'll be reviewing some open cases and suspicious activity in the area. Now enough talk, let's make our way to the bedroom."

"Winston, do you know what time it is? It's way too early to go to sleep."

"Exactly, babe. I never said anything about sleep."

Secret Agent Man

WINSTON ARRANGED TO MEET HIS FBI CONTACT DOWNTOWN AT the US Attorney's office. Part of the package the generals had set up for him was to have access to all US facilities. A gruff-looking man in his late fifties and wearing a dark gray suit showed up exactly at ten. It felt uncomfortable for Winston to use standard twelve-hour time, but he was now in law enforcement.

"You must be Winston."

"Yes." He almost said yes 'sir' but held back. At first, Winston thought the man seemed docile and unimpressionable, but his reputation preceded their meeting.

"I'm Terrence Crowley, everyone calls me Crowley. But you can call me whatever is easiest to remember."

His deadpan smiled seemed FBI-appropriate. "So Crowley, tell me what's on the front and back burners."

"First up, a judge in town is extorting defendants, shaking them down for drugs. Does that sound like something you want to be included on?"

"Yes, but have you talked to Lang?"

"Of course. You have the sanctions to do what the FBI can't. From what they tell me, you have a great amount of latitude regarding your approach to the law. You can devise your own methods."

"Kind of."

"Well, I won't ask. But when you bring a case to me, from that point it has to be by the book. Once I get involved, I need clean evidence that could stand in court."

"Got it. Let's say I'm aware of a particularly evil person; any problem with me running him out of town?"

Crowley shook his head. "No."

"Sometimes bad people seem to get hurt around me."

"Accidents happen all the time. We're going to get along fine. Being a law-and-order guy, I can appreciate your concept: stop the bad guy first, arrest later. I wish we had that mandate. Now that we understand each other, let me fill you in on Judge Ronald Shulman."

Crowley gave an account of the situation. The previous month, a successful Lexington businessman had been arrested for holding several grams of coke, and he was not new to the system. The perpetrator wanted a deal. He could provide federal agents with a dirty judge—Shulman. The informant had been busted three years prior for methaqualone, but the case was dismissed. He claimed that the judge had taken him into chambers and told him the charge would disappear if he provided him with Quaaludes. The man had walked.

Winston's perception told him that the informant was probably believable. Further, if a judge was that dirty three years ago, most likely he was still getting away with it. But Winston knew it would be difficult to get a federal judge to issue a surveillance warrant on a fellow judge, based only on the word of a drug dealer looking for a plea deal. The issuing judge would need credible corroborating facts to validate a criminal informant. He would demand sworn testimony from an upstanding citizen who was above reproach. Then authorization would be forthcoming. "I'm on it, Crowley. Give me the file. I'll let you know when I find what you need. What else do you have?"

"We have over two hundred missing person cases in Kentucky from the last three months. Missing person reports on teenage females are increasing rapidly. I suspect most are runaways. However, at least ten percent are kidnapped victims according to our statistics."

Crowley handed Winston a box with files for the current year. "My regional office specializes in this area. We believe that if you don't find them in seventy-two hours, the chances diminish exponentially by the hour. There is little chance any child will be found from previous years."

"I agree," said Winston. "The first twenty-four hours are key. If you don't have a lead, it usually ends badly. My experience tells me most of the lost children are put into the sex slave trade overseas."

"Overseas?"

"Yes. Even though a sizable number of young girls and some boys are trapped here in the US, typically within driving distance of their hometowns, most are sold abroad. Our resources paint a picture of foreign involvement on a global scale. I'll review the documents with my team."

"A team? I was told you work solo."

Winston played this close to the chest giving Crowley limited information. He respected Crowley's years on the job and was reluctant to reveal material that might lead to unanswerable questions.

"A little of both. I work alone in the field, but I have backup support from state and local police. Also, I have a small group that does research for me and others in similar jobs."

"There are others like you? And what other things?"

"We have regional support for two other metro areas. And we use sources the FBI doesn't."

"You mean like Criminal Investigation Service?"

"No, I mean like psychics and mediums."

"I've read about that, but have no firsthand knowledge of them. What is your experience with all that nonsense?"

"It's not nonsense. In fact, I have extensive familiarity; I'm married to a former CIA psychic."

"Sorry, no offense. Like I say, I don't know anything about that. I'd like to meet her."

"I'm sure you will."

"I don't get to Hopewell often."

"I see you've done your homework."

"Always, I'm FBI. I want you to come to Indianapolis when you can; it's a three or four-hour drive at the max. From what I was told, you're not used to slumming it like us. I guess in the past, transportation was arranged."

"We had Air Force and Navy jets at our disposal. But sometimes we traveled low class in a stretch limo," Winston laughed. "I'm kidding. I've driven the I-95 corridor many times. Do you have any connections with state police for faster travel?"

"Yes, here is an envelope with the various names you'll need, as well as several safe houses to be used as needed. We have access to the governors of Kentucky, Ohio, and Indiana. Now let's stop talking shop and I'll take you to Billy's Barbecue for lunch. You can tell me more about your psychic wife."

Rescue Me

WINSTON RETURNED HOME AFTER HIS MEETING WITH CROWLEY. With his new state police contacts, he was able to travel fast. This worked out perfectly for him to try out his 1980 classic Mercedes-Benz SL 450, with the white and beige interior. When he arrived, in his typical way, he went for the laugh and yelled, "Lucy, I'm home. What's for dinner?"

I yelled back, "Well, Ricky, your favorite Cuban chicken. Fred and Ethyl are joining us." He walked into the kitchen, kissed me hello, and placed two large cardboard boxes filled with file folders on the dining room table. He seemed okay to be working with Crowley, which made me feel good about it also. I was worried that an older FBI agent may be too set in his ways to be receptive to Winston's ideas. The boxes, full of cases, were intriguing enough to get Winston's juices flowing.

"He told me to pick any case I wanted and start working on it. Call if I needed help. He kind of reminds me of Tuck."

Winston had rarely mentioned Tuck, so it piqued my interest when I heard that. Tuck had been a mentor and friend to Winston from the first day he was recruited. Tuck was special to me as well. The night Tuck appeared to me, the Bogota ambush, was a defining moment. I had seen the scene as if I were there. That night and its aftermath had become the fabric of our lives.

Winston had often said that if it were not for me, no one would have made it out. I always wondered what Tuck's family was told about his death. It seemed like a good time to ask.

"After Bogota, what was the official statement to Tuck's family about his passing?"

"A cover story was fabricated quickly. Tuck went missing during a storm while sailing and presumed drowned. You don't bring a body with forty or more bullets in it home to a family without blowing his cover. I missed Tuck every day for a long time. Tried to become him."

Winston had indeed become Tuck. By the time he had left Meade, he was the senior covert agent with the most experience. Everyone had admired him for his dedication to the fight. I believed that Tuck knew Winston was the future of the agency. When he placed him as far back as he could, he was protecting their most valuable asset. Winston had felt guilty at first. He had eventually come to terms with that day, even though he seldom acknowledged it.

"Crowley gave me an invitation to visit Indianapolis anytime and let me shadow him. He wants my perspective on a few things he's working on. Invited me for a round of golf or fishing."

"Did you tell him you don't fish or golf?"

"I told him no. Said if he wasn't too old, we'd play some hoops. But I have no interest in hanging out in Indianapolis. We left the big cities behind us. I like chillin' here in Hopewell with my favorite gal."

"Favorite? I better be your only gal. Oh, before I forget, Dr. Head and his parents will be in Lexington next week. They're coming for the end of the Keeneland meet and staying through the Derby. He wants his parents, who are in their nineties, to have a session with me. His father has a bad hip and is trying to avoid surgery, and his mom has some physical issues too."

"He's sure been a big promoter of yours."

"He has been. I never thought we'd be so close. Are you aware of how well-connected he is in Kentucky, in the horse business and art community?"

"Yes, I've known him a lot longer than you. I think it was cool he bought your first two paintings. I meant to ask you how it went the other day with his friend, Myra?"

"It went very well. I gave her a reading and a healing. As she was leaving, she spotted the large yellow and white painting, *Golden Light*, and bought it on the spot. She's going to hang it in her bedroom. It reminded her of the peacefulness of her grandmother, who loved the color yellow. She's keeping my artwork in mind for her clients."

"I'm so proud of you. You're on a roll, and if you keep on selling your art at this pace, there will be no need to take the school gig, and I can quit my day job."

"I wish, but I don't think you'll ever quit, regardless of how successful I am. Myra said how amazing my healing room and studio looked. Coming from a well-respected designer, that's quite a compliment. Her home and design work have been featured in *Sophisticated Living*. She loved the tufted fabric ceiling above my table, the quartz tabletop, and said my Egyptian artifacts gave the room a warm, spiritual ambiance."

"And, honey, did you tell her who gave you those ideas and who hung the cloth?"

"I gave you the credit. I told her my husband had a soft, inner creative side."

"Let me know when you confirm what day Dr. Head will be here. I'll plan to be at home. Don't want to miss the old coot."

"Yeah, he was sorry he missed you the last time. I'll do my best to pin him to a day and time, but you know the Frenchman."

IN THE MIDDLE OF the night I woke up abruptly, breathing fast, heart racing, and generally feeling uneasy. I left the bedroom to go write a few words down in my journal so I would remember it in the morning.

3:11 a.m., *April 24, 1980- US helicopters crashing and burning in a desert. Iran. Rescue mission. Multiple deaths. Bodies burned.*

The night before, the news had been dominated by the Iranian hostage crisis coverage. Winston and I had discussed President Carter being a good man, a former Naval officer, but wondered why our fellow citizens hadn't been liberated. I did not know if my dream was related to current events. I was tempted to wake Winston but decided to wait until morning. It took me a while to fall back to sleep and I slept later than usual. When I told Winston of the dream, he wanted to act on it immediately, regardless of whether it might only be a nightmare.

He called General Lang and relayed my vision. The general passed the information on to the president, who knew there was a mission in motion. Delta Force had just launched Operation Eagle Claw. Eight choppers had been sent to rescue the American hostages being held in Iran. The president ordered the mission to be scrubbed, but unfortunately, communications weren't instantly received. The copters were too far in to abort. The site commander, responsible for the safety of his men, felt it was too dangerous to evacuate without first deploying air-to-surface missiles to the predetermined locations.

When Winston and I heard about the outcome—eight US soldiers had died from two helicopters crashing into each other during a sandstorm—we each knew what the other was thinking. If I hadn't waited until the next morning to say something, the result might have been different. Winston put his arms tightly around me and said, "Never forget Bogota. Next time, wake me."

After his warm embrace, I went to my healing room to think, pray, meditate and do hands-on healing on myself. I questioned if psychic intellect was a curse or a gift, a faculty everyone has to some extent, but when the ability is heightened to extraordinary degrees does it become a burden? How do you turn the voices and visions off?

After thirty minutes, I left my sacred space, went to find Fred and Ethyl, and retreated to the porch with a glass of cabernet.

God Only Knows

BEFORE I HAD THE OPPORTUNITY TO MAKE PEACE WITH MY mother, she died. On Wednesday, May 7ᵗʰ, 1980, she fell and hit her head on the concrete and had a brain bleed.

Her visitation was held on Saturday at the Hinton-Turner funeral home in Paris. I wore a light blue linen top, off-white long skirt, and a soft pink scarf. Winston thought my choice of dress was rather atypical of mourning attire. He was probably right, but it was what I had been led to wear. We arrived fifteen minutes early, when the doors were opened only to family members. The preacher, my brother Luke, the executor of the estate, and his wife Terri were there. Thomas sat outside in a truck and my sister chose not to attend. The funeral director asked if we wanted to have a private viewing of my mother before they closed the casket. I said no. After making small talk with the preacher, we were told the coffin had been closed, and we went into the viewing room. On top of the box lay a baby blue quilt, the infamous one that my mother had given to me and had stolen back.

When Luke and Terri came into the room, I politely said, "That's my quilt," and quickly added, "well, it's mine if it has a small tear in one of the corners." I remembered the time I had nailed it on the wall as a wall hanging, a big *faux pas* for works of art. Terri reached down to the corner where the tear was. It was mine, alright. Luke said that

Mom had requested in her memorial wishes that this particular quilt be placed over the coffin, and that I could have it back after the burial if I came to her funeral. Terri pointed out that I was dressed in the same colors as the quilt. It had seemed odd that I had chosen those colors, but now we knew why.

The next morning, we attended the funeral before going to the graveside service. My sister, Winston, and I reached Hinton-Turner two minutes late. Initially, we had planned to skip the memorial and just go to the Lexington Cemetery, but at the last minute, we decided to go. When we arrived at the door, it was locked. A gentleman heard our knock and opened the door slightly and said the service had begun and no one could enter. I said we were family. I wanted to say, we're Betty Ann's wicked daughters you've probably heard so much about. We were allowed in and sat in the adjoining room until we were guided to the family room. I had a front-row view of my quilt draped over my dead mother's casket.

The service consisted of a Baptist minister telling stories of Mom, some totally incorrect or foreign to her children, and oddly there was no mention of our father, who was in a nursing home. A distant cousin sang "Amazing Grace," and the Bible passage "for everything there is a season" was read. At the conclusion, there was a limousine to take the family to the cemetery.

Thomas, Luke, and Terri rode in the family car. My sister, Winston and I, opted to drive our own cars. The burial service was short and quick. The quilt was removed from the coffin right before she was put in the ground. Luke folded it into a square and handed it to me at the end of the service.

My mom had trumped me from the grave. She had had the last word. I had to give her credit for her strategic thinking and putting literal meaning into the saying, "Over my dead body." Not only did I come to her funeral, but I also came to visit her on Mother's Day. I had to believe she somehow planned that too.

Born In The U.S.A.

I WOKE UP EARLY, WHICH WAS UNUSUAL FOR ME. THERE WAS NO sign of the sun. Several months had passed since my mother's death, and I felt stronger and more in control of my life on all levels, emotionally, mentally, physically, and spiritually. I didn't really grieve the loss of my mother because I had grieved most of my life over the relationship that we never had. After learning more about borderlines, I had grown to have compassion for their tormented lives, and I understood better their effect on their children. My mother had done the best she could under the circumstances of dealing with an undiagnosed mental disorder.

I predicted I would hear from her fairly soon from the afterlife, either through an astral dream or mediumship. I was in no hurry. She was now released, and hopefully at peace. I knew I was.

Winston had just poured a second cup of coffee when I came into the kitchen. He had fed the dogs and was reading the *Herald-Leader*. Another missing girl was on the cover. This was getting to be all too regular. Winston recognized it was time to convince Crowley that they needed to step up the fight against child kidnapping. They could no longer simply take in the report and check all the appropriate boxes.

Winston put the newspaper away. "Crow's still eager to work.

Most agents burn out or grow cynical after thirty years on the job."

"About time."

"What do you mean?"

"Crow. You finally gave him a nickname; he must be growing on you."

"Yeah, now that I've gained his confidence in my ability to size up a situation and do what's needed."

Winston's first assignment with Crowley already had the corrupt judge on his way to jail. Winston got a statement from a former female NSA agent who had witnessed Shulman take a couple of Quaaludes out of his desk drawer, pop one in his mouth, and offer her one as well. She had faked taking the pill and kept it for evidence. Stamped on it was the name of the company that produced the drug, Lemon 714. It was enough corroboration to obtain a surveillance warrant.

In the judge's chamber, a camera eye had been placed behind his desk in a flagpole that captured images directly over his right shoulder, a surface mic put under his desk, and a dynamic mic positioned in the light fixture above his head. Shulman's egregious behavior caught on tape and camera was ample evidence to arrest him, and for him to plead guilty.

Winston imparted more to me about missing kids. "Most end up in the sex slave trade, whether they are runaways or just snatched while they're outside playing or walking home from school."

A haunting childhood memory surfaced as he talked. And this one wasn't about my mother.

"Winston, this feels very personal."

"What do you mean?"

I shared that when I was in sixth grade, two big, greasy-haired men had gotten out of an old van and followed me on my way home from school. They didn't get close enough to catch me, but only because I instinctively cut through a neighbor's yard. When I arrived home, I was noticeably shaking. My dad had asked what happened, and I described the guys. As soon as I told him, he left the house. When he returned thirty minutes later, he said, "Those men will never be in this town again."

"I don't know what he did exactly. But I could've been one of those girls. I sure hope you can fix this!"

"I'm on it. This is why I started HSOS."

"I almost forgot—you have mail from Russia. It came yesterday. I checked, no perfume, so it's not sweet Rissa. It's not in an embassy envelope either."

I handed Winston the letter. His eyes turned angry after opening it. His expression was enough to scare away a pack of hungry wolves.

"What is it, your eyes are on fire?"

"It's from Putin." Winston flashed me a photo. It was a picture of one of my paintings hanging on his wall. The one named *Freedom*.

"I sold it at the Woodland Art Festival, that was only eight days ago."

"Do you remember the buyer?"

"Yes, an elderly woman from Europe who was visiting her granddaughter. She bought the painting because the name and image reminded her of her husband who died in WWII.

"How could he have it … so quickly?"

"He's skillful at what he does. Probably had an operative purchase it and ship it by military transport."

"Did he say anything?"

Winston handed me the note. I read it out loud. "I fondly remember your visit to my apartment. Maybe one day we can be sitting on your wine porch enjoying the sounds of the birds, my friend."

"Oh my God! He knows where we live!"

"And I know where he lives! This isn't over!"

Bang, Bang

WINSTON HEARD FROM CROWLEY ON AN OVERCAST SATURDAY. THEY had intel on three abducted girls in the area. Crowley believed they would be transported by air out of the country that evening. Winston requested a helicopter and arrived at Indianapolis Downtown Heliport within the hour. Crowley had sent his number-one agent, Chris Forsythe, to greet him.

Winston was briefed on the situation. This was the second time in several months that three girls went missing the same day, around the same time. They were all from small towns that lacked trained personnel or quick access to a local FBI office. That's why Crowley's team became involved as soon as they could.

Forsythe and Crowley explained how they had mapped all six cities by taking a drafting compass and protractor and drawing vector lines appropriately. The lines crossed in only one spot, an area in south Indianapolis where there was a biker bar, Big Mommas. Agents were sent to canvass all the areas that the girls were last seen. Two witnesses in different cities remembered seeing an over-sized motorcycle and an old work van. When shown pictures, both recognized the chopper-style Harleys with Devil Riders on the tank associated with a gang that hung out at Big Mommas.

An undercover drug agent named Smitty from the criminal

investigation division had been in the gang for six months. He was placed there because they were using thousands of dollars of coke per night. Smitty was able to make brief contact and confirmed Forsythe's suspicions, that the Riders had the girls. Because he wasn't in the inner circle, he knew little about the whereabouts of the girls. He believed they were already on a small cargo plane scheduled to leave at dark. He wasn't privy to the location and couldn't ask too many questions, as his life would be in danger if the gang suspected anything. The team had less than four hours to find them before take-off.

The girls were all around twelve years old, from different cities, missing less than twenty-four hours. Two were from Kentucky, Paris and Leitchfield. One was from Evansville, Indiana. All three cities were about two hours and fifty minutes from the biker bar.

Winston was unsure if Forsythe grasped the dire circumstances these girls faced if the team didn't intercept the flight. The girls, more than likely, would be ultimately sold to a wealthy Arab for around three million dollars each. They would be sexually abused on an hourly basis when they first arrived by as many as four to six men. They would be tortured regularly with cigarette burns, hot oil and wax, and beaten with canes. They would be forced to perform sex acts multiple times every day, day after day. After a couple of years their life would deteriorate, and they would get too old to satisfy their owners' sadistic fetishes. Then they would be turned out as street whores at the age of fourteen, with no protection.

It was either save them now, or they would have no tomorrow.

Winston realized Crowley and Forsythe weren't used to working with him. He asked them to trust him, that he was good at making plays. The plan was Winston would pose as a California biker, needing to parley with a Midwest gang for a large coke score. He would enter Big Mommas alone, looking to meet with the leader.

Outside would be fifty or so FBI, state police, and local sheriff deputies. The goal was to find where the girls were before dark.

Forsythe spoke up and thought the plan was insane, one guy going up against thirty or so drunken bikers. Crowley wasn't ready to write off Winston's plan just yet. Winston explained his goal: once inside, he would do whatever it took to sit with the president of the chapter. In his experience with bike gangs, they pride themselves on toughness, so the task might be difficult to achieve. If he couldn't get what he wanted quickly, he'd pick a fight with the biggest guy in the room. He could put him down, or out, in a few seconds.

Winston asked for a photo of Smitty to make no mistake in choosing the wrong biker. Forsythe was still concerned about the others overpowering Winston. He didn't have much time, but Winston explained that bikers respect a code of honor. It would be out of character for a gang to interfere with a one-on-one, biker-to-biker fight.

Winston said he had a much better chance of obtaining information once he gained their attention and respect. He thought the leader would identify himself. If not, he'd call him out in front of his followers. Word comes from the top. No member would betray their chief. He had to be the one to talk to because only the boss and a handful of bikers, his counsel, would know the location.

If Crowley and Forsythe had a better idea, Winston was willing to listen to it. He knew if they came in hard with guns and badges, the gang would either lawyer up or fight, and neither option would provide the information needed to stop the plane. Biker-to-biker, they'd talk to Winston before talking to the FBI.

If Winston wasn't out after fifteen minutes, they were to come in cold, ready to go hot. The clock ticked. Winston requested the FBI's undercover vice squad. He needed biker garb and someone to put on temporary tattoos.

With only one hour and twenty minutes until dark, Winston and Crowley's team assembled down the street from Big Mommas. Winston reiterated that the goal was to find the girls in time, not to arrest anyone. They were to come in soft unless the plan blew up. Then all bets were off, and they would have to do what they had to do. Everyone synchronized their watches on his mark. T minus sixty-eight minutes until dark.

WINSTON WALKED INTO THE club and asked, "Who runs this shithole? There's business to discuss with whoever is in charge of this Girl Scout troop." The bar was a typical low-life saloon, complete with trashy waitresses with harshly bleached hair with exposed dark roots. The bartender—big, fat, fiftyish—looked mean. The floor was dirty and tables supported a couple of dozen overweight, drunken bikers. A handful of thugs looked like they spent hours in the gym lifting weights, but no one in the bunch appeared to be in command. For that matter, no one appeared intelligent enough to be a boss. Observant, Winston figured out the inner circle.

"Who the fuck are you?" said a six-foot-six, three-hundred-pound man to Winston.

He'd hoped it would be easier, but like he had predicted, he needed to earn some respect. "I'm the guy that's going to kick your ass if you're not the boss."

"I'm his first lieutenant, and you're one breath away from death."

Winston hit him twice in the throat with quick knuckle punches, then swung around and hit him in the back of the head with a jump roundhouse kick. It broke the man's neck; he died instantly. The bikers were agitated and angry, but like Winston said, their code forbade members from ganging up in a one-to-one biker fight.

"You're a dead man," said the next guy, boasting how he was going to kill Winston, while pounding his left hand with his right fist.

"I don't think so. Are you sure you want to fuck with me? All I want to do is talk with your pres."

"You killed my brother."

"Sorry, dude. You're next, if you don't bring me to the president of this piss ant chapter."

The guy swung at Winston, who without much effort avoided being hit. Winston picked up a chair and ripped the legs off in one swift motion. He took the two legs and jammed them into the sides of the biker's head. Two down.

"This is getting boring. Are you here?" asked Winston. "Are you afraid to talk to me? I offer a proposal from my pres. Maybe you can't read, my vest says angels as in Hell's Angels. It might make both of us a lot of money." That was the ticket. First, Winston had showed strength; now he baited him with greed. The boss would have to confront him or lose face in front of the members.

"Why do you come in my place and disrespect me?"

"I don't mean to disrespect you. I did come in and ask to speak to you. Your guys seem pretty stupid, if you ask me."

"I didn't ask, and you'll pay for killing my brothers."

"Maybe so, maybe not. Are you man enough to conference with me? It could be worth millions, but I only talk to one man, the boss."

"I'm the president. My name is Carman Machiavelli, who're you?"

"I go by Winston Falcon."

"Everybody stand down. Put your guns away. I got this piece of shit. You better bring a damn good deal, or you will be the late Mr. Winston Falcon."

The sergeant at arms frisked him before they headed to the back office.

As soon as they were alone, Winston kicked into attack mode. He didn't give the leader a chance to respond or even realize what was happening. He brutally flew forward into the biker, hitting him in the throat. While squeezing his esophagus to block his air, he said, 'I'm going to ask only one time, where are the girls?'

Winston slightly let up on his grip so Machiavelli could speak.

"Don't know what you're talking about."

Winston recalled his training on how to get information quickly. He remembered that the ear rips off with only eight pounds of pressure. While holding the man by the throat, Winston reached up and ripped his right ear off. The entire bar gasped when they heard the blood-curdling screams. "You are a low-life piece of shit, this is your only chance to survive. Where are the girls?"

The biker reached into his desk to pull out a gun. Winston hit the biker with the heel of his hand, straight in the nose, forcing the bone into his brain and killing him. Three down. The gang could hear everything.

When Winston appeared with Machiavelli's gun, silence fell over the room. The crowd barely moved, no one talked. He knew if he had let the leader live, a fight would've ensued. Without the leader and enforcers, they were just a bunch of cowardly drunken bikers.

"In ten minutes I bring in an assault team that'll kill every last one of you. Look out the window, dumb asses." Winston turned and grabbed one of the bikers at the head table. "Where are the girls?"

"Don't hurt me! Don't hurt me! They're at Eagle Creek Airport."

"What plane?"

"I don't know. Don't hurt me."

"What plane?"

"Seventy-seven on the tail; I swear, all I know."

The fifteen minutes were up, and the reinforcements came in as planned.

Winston was still holding a biker when he turned to his team and said, "Cuff him. He's coming with us. If the girls leave, he dies."

They drove to the airport in twelve minutes. T minus twenty-seven minutes until dark.

Winston grabs the biker by the throat and said, "Where's the plane?"

"Far end of the field."

"I don't see any with a double seven."

"Wait, I'm wrong. I'm scared. It must be the other end. You're crazy, man. Don't hurt me."

"Is that your group's motto, don't hurt me?"

WINSTON WAS WIRED TO be in touch with the rest of the team. "Winston, it's Crowley, we have the plane in sight. Forsythe is assembling his men to surround it. Drive to the north end."

"I see you; I'll be there in a minute."

Winston grabbed the handcuffed biker. "If the girls make it, you go back to the bar. If they fly off, you die right here on the airfield. I'll leave you cuffed to the steering wheel. Pray you see the girls come off.

"Crow, where are you?"

"I'm on the tail about twenty-five feet back."

Winston said on the radio, "Pay attention, everyone. The pilot knows he can't take off; he sees what's happening. We have to control the scene tightly, so he doesn't do anything stupid that'll get him killed, putting the girls in jeopardy. Forsythe, use your bullhorn to read him his rights, tell him we're boarding. If he moves, he'll be shot.

"Crow, you get the cargo door latch, I'll jump in on three. Forsythe, you tap the windshield on three, so he is staring straight into your twelve-gauge shotgun. Everybody ready, one, two, three."

Winston boarded the plane and disarmed the pilot as Crowley entered. The pilot, shaken and scared, thought he was caught with no escape and gave up quietly.

"Crow, you got him, I'll set the girls free. Bring on the rescue unit. The first thing I want those girls to see is a warm, smiling, female face in uniform. They've been terrorized enough."

Three female state police approached the plane. Winston opened the trunks that contained the girls. They were deplaned and taken to the hospital.

"Listen up," said Crowley. "I want all personnel to head to Big Mommas and arrest everyone on kidnapping charges. My team will take the lead; all the others support, show enough strength in numbers to assure they'll comply. No heroes, no bloodshed. Let's take them as peacefully as possible."

Crowley, with everybody gone, addressed Winston. "It's you, me, and the pilot." In front of Winston, he shot and killed the pilot.

"What the fuck. Why did you kill him?"

"I had to shoot him; I don't want him to witness me killing Robert Sexton."

"Holy fuck, you're working for Putin?"

"You're right, comrade."

Winston knew he had little chance of getting out of this. Distracting a veteran law man would be next to impossible, but still, he had to take a chance.

"Why, why would you betray me, your country, and most of all yourself? You've been on the right side of the law all your life. Lang has known you for thirty years. He and everyone else said you were a straight-up guy." Winston sensed that Crowley was struggling with this decision. In an attempt to stall, he asked, "If you're going to kill me, at least tell me why."

"Somebody was going to take the contract and succeed. I need the money. Sorry."

Terrence Crowley pulled the trigger and shot Winston Forester in the head. Winston plummeted to the ground.

Crowley radioed for an ambulance and called Forsythe.

"Forsythe, change of plans. Put Smyth in charge; you return immediately. Winston has been shot by the pilot. It doesn't look good. How far out are you?"

"Four minutes."

"I need you to come back and work the scene. I'm going to the hospital with Winston." That left Crowley enough time to stage the scene to make it look like the pilot had pulled the trigger. He carefully put the gun in the dead man's hand and re-enacted the shot so the gunshot residue would blow back on the pilot. He had one thing left to do.

"Sally, this is Crowley, I'm afraid I have bad news."

Is This My Destiny

AFTER CROWLEY CALLED SALLY, HE CALLED GENERAL LANG. A CAR was arranged for Sally. Within minutes of arriving at the Bluegrass Army Depot in Richmond, a copter was dispatched and headed for Indianapolis.

"Mrs. Forester, can we get you anything? We'll land at St. Vincent's Hospital in less than thirty minutes. They radioed, and a group of your Fort Meade friends is en route to join you. They're forty minutes out."

"Thank you. I'm fine."

Sally was everything but fine. She was trying to hold it together. The helicopter was so loud, she couldn't think. Her thoughts were going in every direction. She knew Winston might be dead before they landed. Simultaneously talking to herself, praying incessantly, sending long-distance healing, she reached into her purse and pulled out the sacred sistrum, which she had secured before leaving the house. As she shook it in short, sharp, rhythmic pulses, light abruptly emanated from the secret chamber. The papyruses were glowing. She remembered Sabria's words, 'The ARC will find you in the right place and time.'"

As she seized the scrolls, they seemed to come alive. They opened by themselves. Suddenly she was holding the Living Sea Scrolls, unfurled, and about three feet long.

She began reading: *Sally Olivia Stone, it's time. The Living Sea Scrolls have found you. Today you become the latest in a laconic line of chosen healers to carry this weight* ... The scrolls read as if they were speaking directly to her in real-time.

Only the pure of heart will possess the power of the anechoic reception chamber. Now that they have found you, you cannot refuse this. If you misuse it, you lose the strength and endure the consequence of the pain of death. The power is derived from the Hand of God.

You cannot choose when to use the force, it's God's will. The powers bestowed here will only work on those that are Worthy. Be forewarned you can never doubt the supremacies of the ARC. The Creator's energy may flow through you. To become a God Vessel, you must be willing to do whatever is asked of you.

The wisdom texts explained that the Almighty speaks to the ARC healer through a frequency of thirty-three thousand hertz. No human on earth can hear frequencies that high. Like all frequencies, the ARC travels on vibrations.

Sally Olivia Stone, you are the one at this time that can receive this frequency and hear God's voice.

The text defined an anechoic frequency as a direct reception from the source without any echo or reverberation, pure and extremely clean. The chosen listener can only hear it. Thus, the name ARC: anechoic reception chamber. The scrolls listed the chosen healers since the beginning. At the end of the thirty-three listed, was her name.

Hippocrates... Jesus...Avicenna... Jeanne d'Arc ... Sabria... Sally Olivia Stone.

The Living Sea Scrolls decreased in light and slowly curled back into a cylinder shape. She placed them carefully back into the base of the sistrum, and into her purse.

Upon landing, she was escorted quickly to the operating room.

"RIGHT THIS WAY, Mrs. Forester, this is our best neurological team. Dr. Richard Mann is Chief of Surgery."

"Mrs. Forester, here's what we know. Your husband is barely alive. He has a bullet lodged above the medulla, between the cerebellum and the corpus callosum. He appears to be in a coma; however, we don't believe there's brain activity. It's inoperable. If we remove the bullet, a brain bleed will ensue, killing him instantly. If we don't remove it, soon the back pressure from the dammed blood vessel will eventually burst, also killing him instantly. We need to know how you want us to proceed."

"Please, I need to see him and be alone with him. I'll let you know shortly."

"Of course, Ma'am, you have time to say goodbye and pray. However, you only have, maybe, one hour before the superior cerebellar artery will burst."

"Thank you, doctors."

SALLY ENTERED THE OPERATING ROOM. She was aware that with Winston motionless, the abounding serenity engulfing him made the room feel more like a mausoleum than an operating room.

"Winston, my love. I'm here. I know you can hear me. I understand what I have to do. The scrolls have found me; this is the time and place. I'm not afraid."

Healing Hands

WHEN SALLY LEFT WINSTON'S SIDE TO NOTIFY THE DOCTORS about her decision, she was greeted with warm hugs and embraces. Gloria, David, Roger, and Dr. Head were all there. Crowley, present too, was introduced to the group as Winston's friend and FBI director of operations. Of course, General Lang and Crowley recognized each other.

"Crowley, it's good to see you again. I wish it was under better circumstances."

"I couldn't agree more, Roger."

"Sally, I speak for the group," said Dr. Head, "when I say we're all here for you, we're in your corner. Michelle wanted to come also, but I told her to stay and act in my capacity. I spoke with the doctors, and we know what we're facing."

"Thank you, it means so much that you are all here."

Dr. Mann spoke. "Mrs. Forester, have you made a decision?

"Yes. I want to thank you all for what you've done, however, I'll take over now. Excuse me, I must go back to Winston."

The doctors tried to coerce Sally to reconsider.

"You've already stated there's nothing you can do," said Dr. Head.

"True, and we certainly understand and accept her decision.

However, there may be one option left. We have just made contact with one of the world's top neurosurgeons. If we can drill and relieve the pressure and keep the patient alive until he arrives, he may be able to perform surgery."

"There is no time for that, let her be," said Dr. Head. "She has the angels on her side and the wisdom of the ages guiding her. If anything can be achieved here, it shall be done through her. I have seen her miracles before. I ask you to pray with us, and that there's at least one more miracle inside her."

"We will abide by her choice," the doctor said. "We will be standing by to offer any assistance we can."

Sally walked away from the doctors, headed directly into the operating room. She seemed to know what lay ahead for her and Winston. Before she entered, she pulled David aside. "Regardless of what you may see or hear, don't let anyone enter."

David nodded with an enlightened expression and said, "Sally, you were born to do this."

She entered the stark, sterile room and approached the operating table on which her beloved lay motionless and barely breathing. She leaned over, held his hand, and in a soft whisper uttered in his ear, "I am ready." Those who were watching through the observation glass sensed she was already communicating with Spirit.

As if a switch were turned on, a vibration in the room started, gradually increasing until the room shook violently. Walls started to crack; lights flickered and went off. An emergency battery light kicked on. Everyone watched and stared in amazement as Sally quivered ferociously, her hands stretched over Winston. The speed of the vibration continued to increase. Her body trembled and convulsed so intensely that she was blurred to the vision of the five onlookers. She spoke a language no one could understand. In her mind, she was saying, *Heal this child of God,* over and over. What the onlookers heard was more gibberish than any language they knew. Dr. Head discerned it wasn't Latin; he thought it might be a Greek dialect spoken by the Ptolemaic Dynasty of ancient Egypt.

Sally's hair had turned white. Her face was distorted, much like someone faced with hurricane winds. Blood droplets from the corners of her eyes ran down her cheeks. The hallway in which the onlookers watched was amazingly calm. The five became so fixated on what they saw that none spoke or turned away. Finally Dr. Head said, "God is running through Sally. We're witnessing a miracle."

David turned to Gloria, "You were the first one to see Sally as a healer. I remember vividly when you made that declaration during the initial tribunal hearing to see if we were going to accept her as an agent. You predicted then what we're now witnessing."

Twenty minutes into the ritual, the scene continued to attract attention. Twenty-five or more doctors, nurses, and staff peered through the windows. Spontaneously, unsolicited prayers broke out in the crowd. Everyone knew they were witnessing a spiritual event. Suddenly everything stopped. The lights came back on. The room was inexplicably serene. Sally brought her hands together in a prayer position, and bowed her head, as if she was expressing gratitude to a divine presence. Then she collapsed on Winston's chest.

Several doctors, along with Dr. Head, rushed into the room.

Dr. Mann instructed, "Grab a gurney. On three—one, two, three." They lifted her on the gurney and placed her next to Winston.

"Get me Dr. Michaels immediately."

"RICHARD, I CAME AS QUICKLY as I could, what have we here?"

"One for the books" said Dr. Mann. The patient is Sally Forester. Passed out, bleeding from eyes, ears, and mouth. Steady pulse, seems to be in more of a deep sleep than a coma."

"What precipitated this condition?

"I believe she …"

"She just performed a miracle." Dr. Head interrupted the chief of surgery. "I believe what we're beholding is the aftermath of God running through her body. She removed a bullet from her husband's head with her magnetic fingertips, simultaneously stopping the brain bleed."

Dr. Mann looked at Dr. Michaels. "What he told you was as good an explanation as I can think of. I, along with all the others, witnessed this event. See if you can figure out how to stop her bleeding."

Dr. Michaels examined Sally and ordered an MRI. For no apparent reason, Winston, still in a deep, sleep-like state, reached out to Sally and touched her hand. The team was about to witness another supernatural event. As their fingertips touched, sparks erupted, similar to those seen when car battery cables are hooked up. Sally awoke with no signs of blood or pain, just extreme weariness from near-fatal exhaustion. The doctors needed to examine her, so they wheeled her to the triage area outside the operating room.

Word of the miracle had spread quickly. Besides the original five, the neurological team, and the doctors and nurses that observed the phenomenon, there were fifty or more crowded into the hallways to be closer to the spiritual incident. The crowd was buzzing with the story of what had happened. Everyone wanted to see the "angel girl."

"Sally, are you okay?" asked Dr. Head.

"I think I am. How is Winston?"

"He hasn't woken up yet, but he reached out to you and touched your hands. Lie quietly here while we check you out. Tell me what you experienced while you were alone with Winston."

"Dr. Head, I wasn't alone. The loudest noise I ever heard filled the room. Didn't you hear it?"

"No."

"It was a high-pitched frequency that rang like it might shred my ears. The room was vibrating so fast it was difficult to stand. God said, 'Don't be afraid, stretch your hands over him; I'll use you to heal him. Let my light flow through you.' My body filled with what felt like electricity. It was the power of the Creator I was feeling, as I was directed to move my hands over Winston's face and heart. God was testing me while healing Winston.

"The extremely high-pitched sound continued to crush my ears. It felt like having a pencil shoved in each ear; the pain was close to unbearable. I struggled with every bit of my strength to stay in the room. I was determined to save Winston, so I gathered my force from within my heart and was able to give my body and soul as asked. The more I complied with God's command, the less pain I felt until there was no more discomfort. I heard, 'Reach out and touch the wound, the bullet will come to you.'

"As it was decreed, with a loud swooshing sound, the bullet slid out of Winston's head into my magnetic fingertips. I was directed to touch his forehead with the other hand. I complied and the entry wound disappeared. I sensed Winston's spirit fill his body and the loud noise turned into a peaceful, mellow song of birds and others of God's creatures. My psychic powers of vision were restored, I knew Winston would be all right. Afterward, I was given a truth, seen through the hawk's eyes. Dr. Head, it was Crowley who shot Winston. He also shot the pilot and must be arrested. He's an assassin for Putin. You have to believe me."

"Yes, of course." Dr. Head motioned for General Lang to come in and whispered in his ear.

"I'll take care of this," the general said to Sally. "I'll keep an eye on him. There are too many civilians around to act now. Crowley isn't going anywhere. Concentrate on gaining your strength and let's wait for Winston to awaken."

"No, we need to act now," said Sally. "Winston is still in danger.

We must keep Crowley away from him. He'll kill him to keep his secret!"

By now the hospital was nearly uncontrollable. Many had filled the area, wanting to either be healed or be near the "angel girl." With chaos abounding, Crowley, wearing his FBI badge, slipped into the room where Winston was resting with only one doctor watching over him.

"Doctor, you're needed outside immediately. There have been multiple injuries due to the unruliness of the crowd."

The doctor went to offer assistance. Crowley turned toward Winston and pulled out a hypodermic needle. As Crowley approached Winston, an angel in vague form appeared.

With a loud, thunderous roar, the angel struck Crowley down with a mighty thrust of a lightning bolt. *"You will not undo the work of God."* The angel turned to the overcrowded hallway and said, *"Silence!"* Some of the onlookers were awestruck, some embraced the wonderment of the event, all stood silently still in reverence of the divine presence.

To all that witness the glory of God's power, be at peace. When you speak of what happened here today, you will be disbelieved by many. Do not let that persuade you to ignore the truth. Miracles happen. Angels, Healers, and Warriors are everywhere. You Never Walk Alone.

Imagine

WINSTON FORESTER RECOVERED FROM HIS INJURIES. HE VISITED Vladimir Putin one more time. We're unsure exactly what transpired during their reunion, but we do know the KGB officer never bothered him or Sally again. Perhaps it was due to divine intervention, or more than likely, Winston's intervention for putting the fear of God into him.

Shortly after their meeting, the painting *Freedom* was donated anonymously to the Tretyakov Gallery, Moscow's premier depository of Russian fine art. With the feud between Winston and Putin seemingly over, Putin went on to pursue a political career. He faithfully wore and openly acknowledged a cross around his neck. He claimed it was given to him by his mother for protection.

After the NSA's twenty-six-year secret was exposed, the agency grew into the most advanced information collection machine on earth—squads of geeks, wizards, scientists, and innovators who sat behind computer screens, keeping tabs on the world. Covert Operations faded and was never disclosed. All evidence was destroyed. The below-ground fourteenth floor became a storage locker.

Because the tens of thousands who worked above-ground for the NSA were able to keep their secret for almost three decades, it was plausible to conceive that the hundred or so covert division agents would carry their Neptune secrets to the grave.

Six presidents shared this *secret within a secret*: Harry S. Truman, Dwight D. Eisenhower, John F. Kennedy, Lyndon B. Johnson, Richard M. Nixon, and James E. Carter, Jr. All were doing what they thought was necessary to keep Americans safe.

Winston left the NSA during President Reagan's tenure and started a music business. He occasionally was asked to give counsel on national emergencies and world issues to sitting presidents and generals. His original HSOS evolved into Homeland Security, which became the pinnacle of America's defense system.

Winston and Sally eventually traced their ancestral lineage. Their journey took them to Domrémy, France, the birthplace of Joan of Arc, and Hampshire, England, the birthplace of Winston's great, great grandfather. They also sailed the Nile in Egypt and visited the pyramids and the sacred sanctuaries, specifically the temples dedicated to Horus the Hawk and to his consort, Hathor. In Dendera, they asked to see the Music and Jubilation Room where the angel girl received the Living Sea Scrolls. According to all sources—Egyptologists, temple guards, tourist guides, native Egyptians—no such room, or Sabria, ever existed under the name or location given or as Sally described. Like Neptune vanished underground at Fort Meade, Sabria and the music chamber vanished above ground in Dendera.

Sally Olivia Stone went on to become a prominent spiritual leader. Presidents, First Ladies, ambassadors, doctors, musicians, athletes, and people from all walks of life summon her teachings, healing, and other services.

Unfortunately, many of the problems during the Cold War continued to exist. Perhaps more enlightened generations will be born, and they will have learned from all the wars and sufferings to find a way to create a harmonious civilization where there is no need for CIA, KGB, or NSA.

Imagine, in the future, all the people mastering a way to merge dark and light energies of opposites, within themselves and others, and create an alchemy of greater wisdom, love, and healing. Not for one country, or ideology, but for humankind. All the people living in peace. No war, no dictators, no secrets, nothing to kill or die for. Imagine.

A Prayer for the World

Of all the spiritual attributes, love is the greatest. Each being and country needs the warmth and support of the universal spiritual energy. Every breath of love taken in opens the way to fulfillment and enlightenment. Every breath of love exhaled opens the way for others. Spiritual love then expands into a powerful energy. The more it grows, the stronger it becomes. This is true of the soul and every nation. The more wisdom, souls and nations attain, the stronger they become.

Every step taken represents a part of the growth cycle. When a step is taken with the love of humankind, the step becomes at one with the universe. When goodness is at the foundation of every step and every breath taken, there is no challenge that cannot be accepted. The heart and soul remain intact when centered on the love of one another and in the love of our Infinite Spirit.

It is in the darkness of fear, that steps are taken toward the destruction of another; war. To turn all darkness into a flowing stream of the light of love would bring an energy too beautiful to describe; peace. May all existing love-light beings share their sparks with all matter. When sparks hit someone or something else, they ignite more sparks. It then becomes a magnificent cycle. For one soul or country to grow in enlightenment makes another soul or country look at its own path. This leads souls and countries to heal and become beacons of light and love.

(Excerpt from *Angel Prayers*. Written and adapted by the Angel Girl)

About the Author

SAMARA ANJELAE is a renowned Spiritual Healer and Psychic-Medium, recognized as a leader in the field by the Windbridge Research Center and the University of Arizona's Veritas program. Samara holds a master's degree in English Literature and is an accomplished painter whose works are found in private collections throughout America and Europe. She is an award-winning author of several inspirational gift books. This is her first novel.

angelgirlandthehawk.com
Facebook.com/AngelGirlandtheHawk